THE BOOK OF SECRETS

Part 1

Faith Mitchell

ISBN: 1537203215
ISBN 13: 9781537203218
Library of Congress Control Number: 2016913984
CreateSpace Independent Publishing Platform
North Charleston, South Carolina

In loving memory of JT.
This book is inspired by true events.

Also by Faith Mitchell
Hoodoo Medicine: Gullah Herbal Remedies

TABLE OF CONTENTS

1

Bemoi
St. Pierre Island
1780

I stare into the water at my reflection and wonder who I am and what I have become. Before, I was an artisan and scholar named Bemoi. Now, I am a slave who harvests rice and is called Big Jack. How did this happen to me?

Tired brown eyes gaze back at me. They are my own, tremendously aged, sad, and barely recognizable. This salty creek I stare into could be made from my tears or the tears of all of us who find ourselves here in this strange and cruel place.

Blurred memories connect my present and past. I remember running through knee-high savannah grass, running for my life. The dry fronds whipped my legs, and blood trickled down them, trailing into the dust. The scarlet tracks made it easier for my foul pursuers to find me, but I couldn't staunch the blood without stopping—which was the last thing I wanted to do. So I ran, even though in all my life I had never seen anyone outrun the traders who sell men into slavery. Their tribe is called the Sorko, and they are foolish pawns of the coastal merchants who buy and sell people like cattle. Don't they know their turn could be next?

With every grunting breath, my chest burned painfully, but I plunged relentlessly through the thick brush. Behind me was my village. Attacked by the Sorko while we slept, it was now reduced to ashes.

I fled this destruction with just the clothes I wore. I had to leave behind my books and amulets, my artisan tools, even my wife, who was torn from my side by the Sorko marauders. I have no idea what happened to her, but I know that I will never see her again. Many of the melancholy tears I shed now are for her and our lost life together. Fortunately, I still see her in my dreams, when I'm not so exhausted that I fall onto my mat like a senseless animal.

I had to leave everything behind me when I fled my burning village...everything except one of my books, a special one that I have vowed with my life to protect. No one in my village knew about it—not my wife, my parents, or my king. The brethren of my secret society have been its guardians since we began counting time. Through all the shifting kingdoms and changing fortunes of my land, we have guarded the book of secrets. Even though the world as I knew it was crumbling around me, I could not leave it behind. I took it with me, not knowing whether I would live or die or what the future might hold.

2

Bemoi

1780

The Sorko patiently tracked me like a lion pursuing its prey, and eventually they caught me, just as they knew they would. When I couldn't run any longer, I fell in my tracks and lay there in the grass, panting and exhausted. That's when the Sorko captured me. One of them grabbed me from behind and clubbed me until I could not resist. Then I was dragged to a hut where I joined other unfortunates. I recognized some faces from my village; others were strangers. We were thrown together regardless of kingdom, language, or clan and sat, shackled and silent, awaiting our fate. The hut stank of sweat, blood, and fear.

That hut was the beginning of my journey to this island they call St. Pierre, my journey to this creek, where I stare sadly into the water and wonder about this man who is called Big Jack. From the time I was captured, I lost my identity. The Sorko called me "dog" and "slave." They beat me because I didn't understand their garbled, grunting speech. What did they know of my ancient culture? They were illiterate and ignorant.

From the hut, we shuffled for days to the coast. The Sorko fed us, because they wanted to make a profitable sale, but otherwise we were whipped and driven like cattle. I kept my book beneath my robes, desperately concealing it from sight.

When we arrived on the coast, I saw the great water for the first time in my life. We had heard of it in our grassy kingdom, but I never dreamed I would see it. The endlessly crashing blue-and-green waves were frightening but also strangely exciting. The air smelled different—sharp and salty—and the people looked different too. The coast was a strange, new world, where I stared in wonder at the first pale-skinned men I'd ever seen and the enormous wooden ships that carried them across the water.

The Sorko passed us off to different men, who shouted in a foreign language and caged us below ground in a filthy, stinking place with stone walls and iron bars. I searched frantically for people from my village, or who spoke my language, and found a few. We stuck together and tried to understand what was happening to us. From time to time, the pale-skinned Europeans selected men, women, and children from our group, and we never saw them again. Where did they go? What would take place when it was our turn?

One day, I was jerked from the darkness of my subterranean jail into the bright daylight and dragged along a sandy path to a wooden dock that was crowded with groups of people. Boards laid side by side led from it to the deck of an enormous creaking ship. I balked at the sight of the terrifying vessel and the surging waves beneath it. One of my captors beat my shoulders with a stick, forcing me to cross the boards, along with other men, women, and children. I looked back at the shore as the blows rained down, knowing I would never see it again.

After all that I had experienced since fleeing my burning village, I had no idea of the hell I would confront on the voyage that came next. We were penned like dogs below the deck and awash in vomit and shit. For weeks, my ears echoed with the monotonous slap of the waves, the creaking sails, the cries of children and their mothers, and the groans of hopeless, dying people. I despaired of ever seeing the sun or of walking on solid ground again. Many people died during those weeks, but I was determined to live, even though I had no idea what awaited me at the end of the journey.

Throughout that hellish time, I kept the book of secrets by my side, hidden under my robes, and I drew strength from my sacred mission to protect it. It had been wrenched from its roots, and now it was going to a new land. Perhaps its ancient wisdom would have meaning there, and my life would be meaningful too.

3

The ship landed in a foreign city they called Charleston, which was hot like my homeland but much greener; it was more like the rainforest than my dry, grassy home. The streets were full of brown-skinned people who resembled me, but I also saw more pale-skinned Europeans than I'd ever seen before. English, which I'd first heard on the ship, was spoken all around me. I understood only a few words, and I struggled to make sense of my new surroundings.

Only a few of the people who had survived the journey with me knew my name. I was an unknown, a twenty-five-year-old man dressed in torn robes, speaking a language almost no one understood. If you knew how to read my facial markings, they told you about my origins and the secret society I belonged to. But for the unknowing, like the Europeans on the ship, the markings were just ugly scars.

In this new land, I was a new man, but not one of my own making. It was soon clear to me that I no longer belonged to myself.

Before the ship landed, we had been shackled again. Then we were led ashore. It reminded me of being beaten and herded by the Sorkos—how long ago was that? It seemed like another life. Shuffling in a sad procession, we were bullied by shouting men armed with sticks and whips to another pen, this time in a tall wooden building.

We were above ground this time, and the streaming, hot sunlight was welcome. Hot, salty breezes blew away the stink of our weeks at sea.

A few days later, I stood on an auction block where, in the same way they would evaluate a cow or horse, white men counted my teeth, prodded my sides, and pushed my robes aside to lift my penis. I refused to look in their eyes and was careful to protect my book. I was sold to a rice planter whose farm was on an island called St. Pierre. Before we left Charleston, he told me he was going to call me Big Jack.

4

Big Jack
1780

Now I am Big Jack, staring at my reflection in the water and remembering the man I used to be. Big Jack, who faithfully protects the precious book of secrets in defiance of the hostile world he lives in.

Despite my sordid circumstances, I find the island beautiful. It is lush, green, and crossed by muddy salt creeks that team with life. The pines and oaks are enormous and strong, their powerful limbs veiled with soft gray moss. It is so very different from my old land—but I have accepted it as my new home.

I live in a small cabin made of oyster shells and clay on the edge of one of the creeks. My book is safely hidden in a corner, beneath a pile of broken oyster shells. I take it out at night when the others are sleeping in their nearby cabins and use a tiny piece of candle to read by. I unwrap my book carefully, like I would a sleeping baby, and squint at its pages, remembering the meaning of the symbols on them and wondering if anything remains of my old world. Some of the other slaves on St. Pierre say that we can fly back home and be reunited with our loved ones. I wish that were true. I haven't even tried.

One night, when I am studying my book, a sound catches my attention. I look up just in time to see one of the wooden shutters of the cabin move. Crossing the small room quickly, I push it open and see one of the local children on the other side. He must have wakened during the night and seen my dim candlelight.

"Big Jack, what you a do?" the little boy asks me in the island patois. I realize that he has never seen a book before and has no idea that I am reading. It is illegal for slaves to read or own books, but for some reason I decide to speak the truth. Perhaps it is my way of holding onto Bemoi, the man I used to be.

"I am reading," I tell him.

"What that is?"

"It is like having a conversation with distant ancestors."

The boy looks at me with confusion. "What do them say?"

"It's not for children!" I tell him sharply. "They talk of life and death."

He stares at me, and I tell him, "Go back to sleep now. Don't trouble yourself with me."

I gather the book up in its woven cloth and wonder about the wisdom of my actions. The child will surely tell his mother what he saw. Am I sowing the seeds of my own destruction?

Word travels quickly on the plantation grapevine. The child tells his mother about talking to me, and word eventually reaches William Southward, the white overseer, that I am doing something strange.

One evening, when I return, exhausted, from the rice field, I see Southward lurking near the door of my cabin. Like a guilty dog, he slinks away quickly when he sees me approaching. Inside, grass and straw from my mattress are strewn everywhere; the mattress has been slashed to pieces. The oyster shells I keep piled in one corner are also scattered and broken. Fortunately, I moved the book a few days earlier to another hiding place—but now I know that I am in danger.

Sadly, I realize that I must keep the book of secrets hidden at all times, lest it fall into the wrong hands. With time, I hope Southward and the others will forget about it, that their memories will fade like a pebble gradually sinking from sight in a flowing stream.

5

Elizabeth
Chicago
The Present

After five years of fieldwork on St. Pierre Island, I'm confident for the first time that I'm onto something big. I feel like I'm on the brink of a discovery that will make my name after way too many years of working in obscurity. It's because of a story I've heard that—as strange as it sounds—could actually be true, about a mysterious and dangerous book of secrets. If this book is what I think it is, my life will be transformed.

I was initially drawn to St. Pierre because of its history, and now it's my passion. This remote island is wild and beautiful—and haunted too, if you believe the local people. Like the other South Carolina Sea Islands, it still has a rich African culture if you dig below the surface and get into the songs, the stories, and the language. For a scholar like me, it's irresistible: a potential gold mine of information that's valuable for its own sake—and can also translate into a successful academic career.

From the time I first heard it, the story about Big Jack and the book of secrets was striking. It was violent, which would be expected on a slave plantation...but also mysterious. At one level, the story was about an African slave named Big Jack who had been killed by his white overseer. Everyone believed this had really happened, that it had taken place somewhere on St. Pierre.

At a deeper level, though, the heart of the story was the song about Big Jack and his book of secrets. And that's where the mystery begins.

Big Jack's story is a grim one, and the warning at the end of his song would frighten most people off, but on me they have the opposite effect. Something tells me that the story is true, and I'm convinced that if I search hard enough I will find Big Jack's book.

I have a theory that in his West African homeland, Big Jack was part of a secret society whose members swore to protect certain knowledge through the centuries and guard it with their lives. I know from my research that some of these societies were even tied to ancient Egypt, through contacts they made when the Sahara desert was smaller and easier to cross. Their members were literate and used special languages to preserve and transmit their knowledge. Secret information like that would be worth protecting with your life, wouldn't it? Even in a violent foreign land where no one respected its worth or could understand it.

6

Elizabeth

I am convinced that Sam Dent can help me find Big Jack's book of secrets.

Sam's definitely unusual, and maybe that's why we've bonded. We're both outsiders on St. Pierre, even though he's lived there for years. Plus, he's interested in my research—and he's interested in me. Over the years, our relationship has gone from casual conversations about folk songs and folk stories to something a little more...complex, and I like that. Since I see Sam only in the summer, I think of him as a secret indulgence that spices up my life. And he's plenty spicy, believe me.

Last summer, I asked Sam if he knew the song about Big Jack. "Everyone here knows that one," he said. "And they know that it ends 'stay away.' Do you know that too?"

"I heard that's how it ends."

"Because of the 'stay away,' they'll probably tell you they don't know anything about it. Are you prepared for that?"

"Why does it say 'stay away'?" He shrugged and began nuzzling my neck.

I pushed him away. "Come on, it's too hot for that again. I need to get something cold." I disentangled myself from his lovely, lean body and went into the kitchen.

When I returned with my drink, I picked up where I'd left off. "Doesn't the warning make you want to find the book?" I asked. "That's the effect is has on me. In fact, I'm determined to find it."

He pulled me down beside him onto the rumpled sheets. "And you aren't worried that something could go wrong?"

"No. Should I be?"

"Well, you're the folklore specialist. You're always saying there's truth in beliefs and superstitions."

"I know," I said ruefully. "But Sam, I think there's something to this story, and I want to find out what it is. Just think about the papers I could write. It could really help me stand out in that snake pit where I teach."

He was quiet for a moment, like he was thinking things over, and then he said, "I tell you what: I'll help you. Let's see if there's any truth to the song."

"Okay," I mumbled, as he rolled on top of me. My drink spilled, and the ice cubes pressed between us were momentary islands of cold before I went back under his spell.

After that, we went out together a few times, trying to locate the plantation where Big Jack had lived. In the miles of St. Pierre's marshlands, it could have been anywhere. We just didn't have enough information.

It's been frustrating, but I'm determined to keep trying, and now I think I'm at a turning point. A couple of weeks ago, Sam called and said he had a new idea about where we could find Big Jack's book.

He said, "Come back in the summer, but don't come alone this time. Bring a team with you. I think this time we might be successful."

"Why?" I said. "What's changed? What did you find out?"

But he wouldn't give his reasons. "Just come back," he urged, "and bring some students with you."

7

Big Jack
1782

I have decided to marry. I will never forget my first wife, who was stolen from me, but I know I will never see her again, and I would like to have a family. In my home country, marriages are elaborate celebrations involving music, food, gifts, and vows, but here on St. Pierre, it is very different. The whites do not condone slave marriages, so our vows are taken secretly and are not respected. Even so, Bina—whom the whites call Patsy—and I are taking this step because we are determined to live as people, not as property.

One fall evening, we jump the broom, as they call it here. We do it secretly, deep in the woods where Southward won't hear. A few of us gather under a tree with one of the elders, who is the witness. Bina and I drink water together from a gourd and then eat from the same pot of rice. We hold hands, and the elder says that we are now joined in marriage. That night, when I return to my cabin with her, I feel complete for the first time since coming to St. Pierre.

8

Big Jack
1783

Six months after marrying Bina, I am planting rice one spring day when one of the women grabs my arm and urgently whispers, "Southward be selling Bina."

How does she know about this before I do? It's the mysterious plantation grapevine that carries information faster than a bird can fly. My heart stops, and I sink to my knees in the mud. It is hopeless to try to stop the sale: the rice field is far from the plantation house, and my objection means nothing to Southward in any case. I feel enveloped in heat and am acutely aware of the buzzing of mosquitoes and distant cries of birds. Perhaps I cry. Eventually, I look up to see that the woman is still at my side.

"Find out where they're taking her," I ask her. She nods.

I lower my head again and pray to my gods to protect Bina, who is pregnant with our first child. My dream of having a family is already being crushed.

A few days later, I find out that Bina has been taken to a plantation on another island several miles away across the salt marsh. It will be difficult to visit her, but I will do that when I can, especially once the baby is born. In the meantime, I am alone again in my cabin. Reading my book would comfort me, but I am afraid to take it from its hiding place. Does it have powers that would help me in this foreign land? I don't know yet. I am so isolated and crippled by fear that my powerful book of secrets is like a sleeping flame, waiting to be reignited.

9

Finch
St. Pierre Island
May 20

"Shit, it's hot," Russell said, getting out of the car at the cottage where we would be staying for the next six weeks.

He was one of those people you could depend on to state the obvious. But I have to admit that I wasn't prepared for the wall of sun and hot air that smacked me in the face when we arrived. Russell Bennett, Sierra Jackman, and I had driven overnight to St. Pierre Island with Elizabeth Wood, the professor of our Black folklore class. It was still late spring when we left Chicago, with small light-green leaves and blooming lilacs, but on St. Pierre it was intensely hot and *green, green, green*. There was no other way to describe it. The road was lined by ancient oak trees that arched overhead, moss hanging like seaweed from their huge, heavy branches. The effect was like entering a dark tunnel into a different world. Lush, grassy salt marshes bordered the road and stretched to the soft green horizon, interlaced with muddy creeks. Wildlife teemed in the air, on land, and in the creeks. Some of it was deadly—to my dismay I'd already seen a dead rattlesnake as big around as my wrist, lying by the side of the road.

After the heat came the smell, like a one-two punch. It was a ripe and overpowering odor that filled my lungs at every breath.

"Jesus, it reeks! What *is* that?" Sierra asked shrilly, and Elizabeth explained that it was salt we smelled, from the grassy salt marshes that separated St. Pierre from the Atlantic Ocean and that snaked alongside the road. Altogether, the island looked, smelled, and felt exotic and vaguely frightening. Everything about it seemed alive, powerful, and relentlessly potent. *This is my world*, the island seemed to say, *and if you want to survive, you have to play by my rules.*

A few minutes earlier, driving down St. Pierre's main road, we had passed a few people walking along the side in the shade of the trees, but we had seen few houses. The people we passed seemed vaguely strange. They were mostly old and dressed in worn farm clothes; some carried hoes on their shoulders. The expressions on their dark, lined faces were closed, and they didn't meet our eyes. One elderly woman even balanced a large woven basket on her head, as though she had stepped out of the nineteenth century.

"Have you guys ever seen something like that before?" Elizabeth asked as we drove past her, and we all solemnly shook our heads. What was this place? What were we getting ourselves into?

"I've got to get a photo of her," Russell said, groping in his pocket for his phone.

"Don't be so obvious!" Sierra snapped, slapping his hand.

Eventually, Elizabeth had pulled into a sandy, rutted driveway that led to a weathered wood-frame cottage painted a faded pink, with blue shutters and a dark-blue door. It might have been nice once—there were carved Victorian designs around the eaves and on the handrail around the small porch—but it looked like no one had lived there for years.

"This is where we're going to stay for the next six weeks," she announced with enthusiasm. We looked around skeptically. Where? Here? In a broken-down little house partially covered in moss and surrounded by looming trees?

"Come on. Let's get moving," she said briskly. "I want to get settled in so that we can have our first team meeting tonight."

"We're working already?" Russell said to no one in particular. Then he tugged on Sierra's arm, and I heard him whisper, "Coming here was your idea. I hope you know what you're doing."

Sierra shrugged and scolded him loudly enough for me to hear. "Come on, Russell. Live a little for once in your life. Try doing something your parents didn't tell you to do."

"Shit," he replied. "Do *your* parents know about this?"

"Well, not exactly. I just told them I was going on a field trip with one of my professors, and that was okay with them."

I wondered how close the two of them were. I only knew them from class. I dreaded the prospect of being the third wheel of a romantic duo.

Elizabeth walked over and broke up their little huddle. "Come on, guys," she repeated. "We need to get moving. The house has electricity, but we have to get our own water from the pump. We have work to do."

"We're pumping water?" Russell and Sierra both asked in dismay. Elizabeth laughed—I thought rather unsympathetically—and walked up the stairs to the blue door.

Meanwhile, I looked around at our new surroundings. Overgrown shrubbery that hadn't been pruned in years surrounded the pink house on three sides. There were a few scraggly plots of flowers too, but untamed nature was gradually reclaiming what had once been a carefully tended yard. Already, part of the roof had caved in, which meant that only part of the cottage was livable. I thought I'd better get inside and claim a space before Russell and Sierra took the best spots.

Just as I was about to go inside, I saw something move on the other side of the sandy driveway. Jerking around, I saw a tall, slim older man emerge from another small house that I hadn't noticed before. It was almost a twin in size and style to the pink one, but the wood was unpainted and a weathered gray. A few tufts of white hair and a patchy beard framed the man's dark-brown face, while his eyes were cloudy with age. He faced in my general direction but looked past me and began talking. In fact, it took me a moment to realize that he was actually speaking to me.

"M-m-my name is Caesar Cummings," he stuttered. "Th-th-these are m-m-my houses." He still didn't look at me, as though his eyes were misfiring along with his tongue. Then he stood perfectly still, and I guessed that he was waiting for me to respond.

"Um, thank you for letting us live here," I said. "Do you live in the gray house, Mr. Cummings?"

As though he hadn't heard me, the man repeated, "M-m-my name is Caesar Cummings."

I realized I'd forgotten my manners and stuck out my hand to shake his. "Hello, Mr. Cummings, my name is Finch Waters."

"P-p-pleased to meet you, Miss Waters," he said.

"You can call me Finch," I offered, and for the first time he looked at me directly. I saw that he was wearing some kind of small amulet on a cord around his neck, and I wondered what it was for.

A little too loudly, I said, "I'm going to get settled in now," as I turned away from the socially awkward Caesar Cummings and started up the stairs with one of my bags.

"Y-y-yes, ma'am; g-g-good d-d-day," he said politely, tipping his head slightly as though wearing an invisible hat.

"Would you like to come in and meet the others?"

"N-n-no," he said, "I be back later," and he turned and walked stiffly back toward the gray house.

It was a strange introduction to St. Pierre, and I was glad to be rid of him. I hoped he wasn't typical of the people who lived here.

Inside, the little pink house was in better condition than I expected it to be, although it was dusty and very hot from having been shut up a long time. There were two porches, a small one in front and a larger one in back, four tiny bedrooms, a kitchen that was attached to the back porch, and a small front room. Another part of the house was unusable because of the collapsed roof. Fortunately, that wing had a door that we could keep closed so that nothing would come walking or slithering into our part of the house.

The house gave me the feeling that Caesar had just left it one day and locked the door behind him, leaving everything in place. Ancient photographs covered in bleary glass ringed the walls of the front room, and personal items like worn hairbrushes lay on tables, as though their owners were about to come back and use them again. Everything was gray with dust.

In the bedroom I'd chosen for myself, I had to push aside the belongings of some past occupant to make room for my own. Confronted with an ancient bed, covered in a faded quilt, I decided to sleep on top of it rather than risk seeing the bugs and God knows what else that had moved into the mattress over the years.

From one of the other bedrooms came the sound of Sierra's occasional shrieks. I figured she was dealing with the dust too, or maybe bugs. If I was struggling to adjust, I could imagine what that delicate soul was going through.

10

Big Jack
1783

I bide my time, sweating in the rice fields from daybreak to sunset, plodding to my cabin like an ox, falling exhausted onto my straw bedding after our communal meals. Others gather around the fire to sing and talk after eating, but I keep to myself, and my heart is as cold and heavy as a stone.

One day, the plantation grapevine tells me that Bina has had a baby boy. I stop Southward the next day, bow my head in the subservient way that he loves so much, and tell him, "Mas' Southward, I would like to visit Bina and my new son."

"You'll need a pass for that," he replies curtly, as though I didn't know that.

"Yes, sir. You would write one for me?"

"No," he says harshly. "Too many of you abuse them. You say you'll come back the next morning and don't return for days. And then I'm the one who pays for it." He turns on his heel and adds over his shoulder, "Besides, I hear you can read, which means you could copy it."

So that is that. We are whipped and branded for overstaying a pass, and Southward is merely reprimanded. But he considers himself the victim! Then and there, I begin making my own plans to visit Bina. I tell no one because someone would surely tell Southward, hoping to use the news for their benefit. What benefit? Maybe a piece of cloth or an extra serving of shit-filled pig guts. That's what some of us have been reduced to.

I leave one night when the full moon makes it easier to see, traveling through the marshes and creeks by canoe and foot, keeping a sharp eye for rattlesnakes and cottonmouths. Once, I spy a fisherman casting his net for fish, but I keep my distance from him. Otherwise, I am alone with the birds and forest animals. For a brief time, I feel like a free man again, roaming the land to find food for my family.

Traveling by night and sleeping by day, it takes me two nights to arrive at Bina's plantation. I creep through the bushes to the slave quarters and meet up with a small group of men who are sitting around a fire. They are not surprised to see me, because they understand what husbands must do—husbands who are separated from their wives. We talk briefly, and then they point me in the direction of Bina's cabin. It is a small one made of weathered wood covered with moss.

I knock on the shutter, and after a few minutes I hear footsteps. Then Bina peers out of the opening warily. Her cautious look quickly melts into a smile, and soon I am standing in the cabin, reunited with my beautiful wife and meeting a tiny stranger, our son. We decide to name him Tolo, a word that means "star" in my language. When I look up at night, I see stars I knew in my homeland. They are still with me, even though my whole life has changed. Stars are eternally free.

I hold Tolo closely, helplessly smiling at his innocent brown eyes and waving hands. What will his future be? I pray that unlike me he will be a free man. After all, he was not captured like Bina and me; he was born in this new country.

"We are from across the sea," I say to Bina, "but our son is an American." We laugh, because no one ever calls the Black children Americans. But in the privacy of our own small world, where we are people, not property, we can say what we know is true.

11

We gathered in the living room for our first team meeting, and Elizabeth started by dropping the news that there was no cell-phone service on St. Pierre.

"Are you shitting me? I'm going to be stuck on this island for six weeks with *no phone?*"

Elizabeth shot Russell a hard look. "We came here to do research, not to chat and text with our friends."

"But I told my parents I'd keep in touch," Sierra whined.

"There's a phone down at Mrs. Taylor's store that you can use."

"Mrs. Who? What store? There's no phone here?"

"Sierra, there's no phone, no running water, and no inside toilet. That's how they live on St. Pierre. You're just going to have to deal with it."

Sierra twisted her face and turned away like an angry child.

"Shit," Russell said under his breath. "You could at least have told us before we got here."

I didn't say anything, but I wasn't happy about the news either. How was I supposed to stay in touch with my parents and friends? Already, I felt like the island was closing in on me.

Elizabeth ignored Sierra and Russell and told us more about our project—*the expedition,* as I thought of it. I was honored that she'd included me on this fieldtrip to St. Pierre Island, and a little nervous because Sierra and Russell were just people I'd met in class. Back in Chicago, Elizabeth had assured me that I'd be okay on the newly composed team. "The three of you will have a chance to bond on this trip," she'd said with a wink.

Without phones, we'll definitely have a chance to bond, I thought darkly.

We sat in a circle, on ancient stuffed chairs that creaked and exhaled puffs of dust when we shifted our weight. I decided to cover my seat with a towel. There was no telling what kinds of bugs called the chair home, and I didn't want to find out the hard way. I'd already seen some disturbingly large roaches scuttling along the front room's walls, and I dreaded the idea of going to bed later. What creatures were waiting to emerge from their hiding places when the lights went out?

"Okay," Elizabeth said, looking around the circle. "What makes St. Pierre distinctive?"

"It has strong African roots?" Sierra ventured. She was often uncertain of herself but was still outgoing.

"You're forgetting to say why," Russell quickly lectured. "There weren't any bridges between St. Pierre and the coast of South Carolina until the 1930s. And because of the hot, damp climate, there weren't a lot of whites. *That's* why the African culture is so strong."

"Anything to add, Finch?" Elizabeth asked me.

"Like the other Sea Islanders, the people on St. Pierre call themselves *Gullah* or *Geechees.* They have their own dialect that is related to the patois that people use in Sierra Leone." Using the word "patois" and saying it correctly made me a little self-conscious in front of Sierra and Russell, but I wanted to show that I had been paying attention in class.

"Not bad, you guys," Elizabeth said. "You remember more than I expected. So, putting it all together, St. Pierre and the other Sea

Islands are very different from other parts of the South. They are known for their language, customs, songs, and stories—including the ones about Brer Rabbit. Those stories Uncle Remus told were from the Sea Islands, and they're the kind of Black history I want to preserve before it's lost forever. That's why I've been coming down here every summer for the last few years."

"Do you have friends here?" Sierra asked.

"Researchers have to be careful about making friends with their subjects," Russell interjected, as though he knew what he was talking about.

Elizabeth ignored him and said, "Yes, there are some people I've gotten to know, but the islanders are very reserved. In fact, at first, it might seem like they're rejecting you, but they're just being careful until they get to know you."

I thought about this. Maybe it explained why people who were walking down the road glanced toward the cottage, but did not wave or come to the front door. So far, there were no signs that we were welcome in the small community. There were no signs of Elizabeth's friends either, but she did not seem to be concerned about that.

I'd begun to notice a slightly familiar scent in the house in addition to the smell of dust, and it puzzled me. I glanced around the small, poorly lit room. Caesar Cummings's long-dead family members gazed back blankly from their gilt frames hung on the surrounding walls. What if they dragged themselves from their muddy graves and decided to reclaim the house? After all, it had been their home... I shuddered and forced myself to focus on Elizabeth and the rest of the group.

"Okay," Elizabeth was saying. "I want to explain what we're going to be doing here on the island. Have any of you ever heard of Big Jack?"

We all shook our heads no.

"Right," she confirmed. "I didn't talk about his story in class because I'm still piecing it together. That's what we'll be doing this summer."

12

Big Jack
1783

Somehow, Southward finds out about my trip to see Bina. I am not surprised. It is impossible to keep secrets in our small world, where there is always someone who thinks they can get ahead by sharing information with whites. Naturally, he wants to make an example of me in order to discourage others from breaking the rules and to remind us of his total authority over our lives.

At his order, I am stripped and lashed to a large oak. The side of my face is pressed painfully against rough bark that digs into my skin. I stare into space, steeling myself for the first biting blow of the whip.

Southward whips me until I can feel the skin splitting over my ribs like tearing cloth. The blood from my shredded back forms bloody rivers that mix with the dust and run off into the grass—just as my blood ran years ago, when I fled the Sorko slave traders. My groans punctuate the slap of the whip. Southward commands the other slaves to watch my humiliation, but when I raise my heavy, sweating head, I see that their troubled eyes are turned away.

Eventually, the ordeal ends. I slump against the tree, too weak to stand on my own. The rough bark that was once so onerous is now a comforting resting place. Pain is all I am aware of. I hear Southward give orders for me to be cut loose and taken back to my cabin. I feel hands dragging me through the dirt. At Southward's orders, other hands run salt into my open wounds, supposedly to prevent infection. I scream like a wounded animal, my lonely cries echoing in the hot, still air.

It takes me months to recover from the whipping, which leaves my back stiff and ridged with welts like thick tree roots. I return to the rice fields and am sociable with the others when I need to be. Mostly, though, I keep to myself. I am biding my time until I can gather up Bina and Tolo and we can escape for good. We will hide ourselves deep in the salt marshes, where no one can find us, and live our lives in peace.

I wait until a long, dark winter night with no moon. It's difficult traveling through the marshes without moonlight, but there's less risk that I'll be detected. I gather my few belongings and unearth the book of secrets from its hiding place. Then I set forth on the journey to free my family.

The first night, I travel without problems through the chilly marshes, carefully making my way by foot and canoe under the shadows of the pine trees. When I think it is safe to do so, I light my way with a fiery torch. At sunrise, I tether my canoe to a tree and build a shelter from brush and dead branches to rest in until nightfall.

The sun is setting and a cool mist is falling on the land when a distant sound disturbs the air. I stiffen, all of my senses on alert. It is a dog—no, several. Their baying voices echo across the water, warning me that they're on my trail. The night before, I crossed several creeks, and now I am hopeful that the water and mud will confuse my scent until night falls again and the search party returns to the plantation. While it is still daylight, I will stay hidden in my brush shelter.

Time passes slowly. The forest is silent except for a few birds. Then, breaking the quiet, there is more baying, and it is much closer this time. I hear splashing and urgent voices that are ominously close.

Southward shouts orders, and Black voices respond. My heart pounds frantically, my chest tightens, and I decide to flee.

I run faster than I ever have before, faster than on that fateful day in my homeland. For a moment, I wonder if I will always be running, if fleeing pursuers is my destiny. Then I force my attention back to the moment. Branches whip my face, and the soft, uneven ground forces me to move adeptly. I am no longer running toward Bina; I am just running for my life. And now I am getting tired. My vision blurs, and the scars on my back begin to tighten and burn, but still I push onward. I know that Southward will kill me if he catches me, so I am a man with nothing to lose.

I trip and fall, just as I did long ago, running from the Sorko. Southward's dogs are instantly on me. They have been steadily gaining on me as I grow increasingly tired. One of them grabs my left leg between its savage teeth and twists its head, tearing my flesh horribly. Another is snarling by my head, forcing me to inhale its foul breath as I gasp on the ground. I am groaning in agony when suddenly my vision goes black, and it feels like I'm falling down an endless hole.

13

Finch
May 20

"Here's what I know so far," Elizabeth said, and she told us a story about a slave named Big Jack and a stolen treasure:

"Big Jack was a slave who lived on a plantation on St. Pierre Island. His wife and child were on another island, across the salt marshes. One day, Big Jack visited his wife without getting a pass. He went off at night and came back two days later before dawn. Now these marshes and creeks are full of rattlesnakes and cottonmouths, so that tells you how much he wanted to see his wife.

"The overseer thought that Big Jack had been sick. Somehow he found out the truth. To punish Big Jack, he whipped him until the skin split over his ribs. After that, Big Jack swore that he would run away for good as soon as he could. What's more, he decided that the plantation owner owed him money for all the work he'd done for him without pay. Big Jack told the other slaves that was only fair.

"One night, Big Jack disappeared again. The next morning, the overseer said that a box of money was missing too. No one knew how much was in it, other than Old Massa, but soon everyone on the plantation knew that a lot of money was gone—'a fortune,' according to Old Massa—and that Big Jack had taken it. The overseer was enraged that Big Jack had outsmarted him, and he used dogs to follow his trail into the salt marshes. Eventually, after a three-day search that he led himself, the overseer found Big Jack where he was hiding, deep in the swamp where he had thought he would be safe.

"The overseer tortured Big Jack to find out what he'd done with the Massa's money. Big Jack never said a word. Even when the overseer began breaking his fingers one by one, he never said a word. The overseer was so angry that he pulled a pistol from his waist and shot Jack, just like that. Then he hacked Jack into pieces with a big knife and dumped the pieces into the creek that ran past the house. To this day, the islanders avoid the spot where it all happened."

"That's disgusting!" Sierra declared. "What a tragic story. Jack just wanted to visit his family, and he ended up dead."

"If I were Jack," Russell added, "there's no way that white man would have taken me down. I would have fought him to *the death*, right there in the salt marsh. If I go down, you go down too."

"Well, that's how the story goes," Elizabeth said, "and I've been told that that there's a song that goes along with it. That's what I want to track down. I want you to help me find a song about Big Jack."

"Do you think that will be hard?" I asked.

"It could be," Elizabeth replied. "At first, people might say they've never heard of Big Jack. You're going to have to be patient and persistent. Ask everybody you talk to."

Somewhere in the little house, I heard a rustling sound. The wind? A snake under the floor? The cottage was raised about a foot off the ground on concrete blocks. Anything could be moving around under there. Russell must have heard the sound too. He looked around nervously, and for a moment his eye caught mine. His face and Sierra's were tight; I wondered if mine was too.

Elizabeth looked at us and smiled reassuringly. "I know it's all a little strange," she said, "but you'll feel better in the daylight. That reminds me—does anyone need to use the outhouse before we turn in for the night? Tomorrow, we'll buy some chamber pots, I promise, and you can make some calls."

An outhouse. Ugh. I still couldn't believe this was how we had to live. Elizabeth should have warned us before we left Chicago!

The outhouse was behind the house, near a patch of trees. "I'm not going out there alone," Sierra declared firmly. "Someone has to go with me."

We decided to go together. Heading out first with the flashlight, I pushed the back door open and stood at the top of the little flight of steps that led into the backyard. There were no lights outside the house that could be turned on. For that matter, there were no streetlights on the road either. The island at night was pitch dark—darker than any place I'd ever been before. Looking up, the stars I could see were brilliant through the restlessly moving branches of the trees. With sharpened senses, I could also hear mysterious rustlings and little sounds, as though we were being watched from the shadows.

I hoped Sierra and Russell wouldn't notice that my hands were shaking. I led them down the stairs and along a little path that I could barely make out in the dim circle illuminated by the flashlight. I felt as though the dark night could swallow me up. What was I doing here? What the hell were any of us doing here?

"I've really got to go, so I'll go first," Sierra announced. "Finch, you hold the light," she directed.

She yanked on the outhouse door, which opened with a groan. God only knew when it had last been used.

"Wait, there could be all kinds of spiders in here," Sierra said. "Finch, give me the light." When she wasn't doubting herself, she could be very bossy.

"If I give you the flashlight, Russell and I won't be able to see!" I objected.

"It's more important for me to see what I'm doing," she countered. "You have each other."

I had Russell to depend on? At that dubious thought, I looked over toward where Russell was standing. I could just barely see him. He tried to laugh, but it wasn't convincing.

Sierra went into the pitch-dark little shed and pulled the door partly shut. We heard her clothes rustling and saw the movements of the flashlight beam as she adjusted herself. Then she gave a sudden, shrill scream. I heard the flashlight hit the ground as we were all plunged into darkness. Sierra screamed again and shoved open the outhouse door, swatting at her body and looking around desperately in the darkness. I could just barely see her frightened brown eyes and the caramel outlines of her face.

"Where are you?" she asked, on the edge of hysteria. She was panting with fear. "Something attacked me!" She began swatting her legs and crying. "My legs are on fire. Help me!"

We huddled by the outhouse door, unsure how to get back to the house. Sierra cried and slapped her legs, while Russell and I desperately called out for Elizabeth. Why didn't she hear us? Couldn't she hear Sierra crying? Just then, a small light appeared from the direction of the house and moved toward us. I sighed with relief. But as the light grew closer, I saw that it was not a flashlight beam, and not Elizabeth, but something greenish and glowing.

As it came closer, I thought I heard whispering voices, speaking in the Gullah dialect. I panicked and started running, with Russell and Sierra right behind me. Where was the door? Where were the stairs? Just then, Elizabeth opened the back door, and we ran toward the safety of the rectangle of light. Now even the spooky little cottage felt safe, compared to the terror outside, and it suddenly felt like home.

Back inside, we saw that Sierra's brown legs were covered with a multitude of tiny, swelling red bites. "Shit," Elizabeth said—I had never heard her swear before—"the fire ants attacked her. First we have to kill them, and then we'll put some rubbing alcohol on the bites. They're going to itch like crazy. That old man should have sprayed this place. He knew we were coming."

Sierra was crying too hard to help herself, so Elizabeth and I took charge of slapping the ants off her legs. Russell stomped on any of them that tried to escape.

"This is not exactly a friendly environment," he commented. "Cottonmouth snakes, rattlers, biting ants...and as dark as the back of the moon. We're going to have to be careful."

You didn't even mention that strange green light, I thought. And so our first day on St. Pierre ended.

14

Big Jack
1783

When I come to, I am lying in the dirt outside my cabin. My mouth hurts, and I taste blood. I can see again, but my vision is blurry, and I have trouble opening my eyes. My head is heavy, and it's difficult to hear. I try to stand, but my left leg is numb and will not respond.

There are muffled sounds in the cabin. Southward emerges, holding the few belongings I took with me into the marshes. He quickly discards my clothes on the ground but has a tight hold on the metal box that I keep the book of secrets in. Grunting, I try to get up on my feet to take it from him, but I am as powerless as a baby. I scream in frustration and writhe on the ground.

Glancing over at me scornfully, he forces the box open with a rock. Inside it, my book is wrapped in the cloth it traveled in across the ocean. Southward unwraps the cloth and opens the book. I don't know what he expects to see, but I can tell from his expression that he is shocked and confused by what he finds. He cannot understand the language of my book, but even so, it's not safe to let it fall into his ignorant hands. That would betray my vows to protect it. I had hoped to teach Tolo its secrets, but what has become of that dream? It is slipping away while I lie here in the mud. I hope that at least my son will remember my name.

Southward is screaming in my direction, saliva flecking his lips. "What is this fucking gibberish?"

I do not respond.

"Explain these devilish signs," he rages.

Again, I do not answer.

Southward kneels and grabs one of my hands. He jerks a finger backward until I feel searing pain and hear the dull snap of the bone breaking.

I groan deeply but say nothing. My forehead breaks out in a cold sweat. I know I will soon join the kingdom of my ancestors. Perhaps I will see my beloved first wife again, too. Forgive me, Bina, for thinking of her, and know that I loved you both.

He breaks the fingers of both my hands, one by one. Through eyes stinging with mingled sweat and tears, I see sorrowful Black faces watching in silence. They are as powerless as I am.

I say nothing.

Finally, I gasp through frothing lips.

"What did you say?" Southward screams. "What? Goddamn you, you ape!"

I am asking the book to protect itself and to punish those who harm me. Foolish Southward thinks I'm trying to tell him something. When I speak again and he can't hear me, he pulls a pistol from his waist and shoots me in the chest.

I feel my body twitch and then come to a rest in the mud. The air stinks of gunpowder, sweat, and blood, but I am at peace.

15

Big Jack
1783

"Fetch me a cutlass," Southward ordered one of the slaves who silently circled Big Jack's still-warm corpse.

When the man didn't move, he flicked his feet with the whip and repeated, "A cutlass!"

Dreading what was to come next, the slave man brought one of the cutlasses used by the work crew to clear away sea grass. Southward seized it and, sweating and grunting, began hacking at Big Jack's mangled legs. Horrified, the other men watched in stunned silence. The sound of the cutlass blows reverberated in the stagnant air under the trees.

Southward continued until Big Jack's body was reduced to a headless torso and his butchered head, arms, and legs lay scattered about him like trash. Red-faced and sweating, he looked around wild eyed at his silent witnesses and ordered, "Dump this shit in the creek."

"What about him things?" one man asked timidly. He was small, with tribal markings that resembled Big Jack's.

"Dump that shit too." But the slaves didn't move.

"Didn't you hear me? Get that mess out of here."

"But Mas' Southward," the small man said, "we a be cursed."

"What?" Sweat still poured down Southward's leathery, lined face, and his drenched body stank like overripe fruit. He panted for breath like one of his dogs.

"Big Jack a say that anyone who touch him a be cursed."

"When? I didn't hear that." The slave men looked at each other, silently confirming Big Jack's words.

"Don't fucking waste my time with that nigger juju. Take him away!"

The slaves remained frozen until Southward furiously reloaded his pistol. Then, they reluctantly loaded the remains of Big Jack into a wooden wagon, making secret protective signs among themselves. When they reached the edge of the creek, they dumped Big Jack's remains overboard. It was the same creek he had fled across just the night before.

Meanwhile, when Southward's back was turned, one of them gathered up Big Jack's book, rewrapped it, placed it in the metal box, and buried it in a corner of the cabin. Fearful of its power, he did not look inside, and he hoped the book would remember that favor.

After Big Jack's death, life on the plantation superficially returned to normal. But among themselves, the slaves were apprehensive. They whispered to each other about Big Jack and felt that something was about to happen. For protection, they marked their cabins with occult signs and wore magical amulets.

Just two months later, a massive storm destroyed the plantation. It came up suddenly from the direction of the salt creek, a tempest of mighty winds and ceaseless, driving rain. When it was over, branches of the pines and mighty oaks lay broken on the ground, tangled up with moss as thick as seaweed. The roof had fallen in on the plantation house, and in the slave quarters, cabins were tossed around like dry leaves. Floods drowned the rice fields, and most of the crop was lost.

An epidemic followed on the heels of the storm, striking nearly everyone on the plantation with fevers and virulent rashes that lasted for days. Southward survived, but his face and arms were scarred for life. Most of the slaves who had witnessed Big Jack's death died horribly, twisting on their straw mattresses with fevers that soaked their ragged clothes and screaming that snakes were crawling beneath their skin.

From that time on, the slaves who survived the storm and epidemic avoided Big Jack's cabin and the place where his body lay. To warn their children and future generations, they composed a song to sing when the whites weren't around:

Big Jack had a secret book
He did; yes, he did
He kept it by his side
He did; yes, he did
He lived beside the water
He did; yes, he did
Where the salt marsh meets the tide
He did; yes, he did
Massa murdered Big Jack
He did; yes, he did
For wanting to be free
He did; yes, he did
He cut him into pieces,
Yes, he did; yes, he did
And threw him in the sea
Yes, he did; yes, he did
Don't trouble Big Jack's secrets
Keep away; keep away
Don't try to read his book
Shut your eyes; shut your eyes
It's a book of fearsome power
Stay away! Stay away!
You'll be cursed if you look
Stay away! Stay away!

16

Finch
May 21

I woke up confused. Where was I? I stared blearily at the old wooden furniture and the plastic hairbrush missing half its bristles and remembered: oh yes, Caesar Cummings's quaint cottage on St. Pierre Island. Well, at least I'd survived the night, although the old cast-iron bed was not exactly comfortable. The mattress felt and sounded like it was filled with straw. Was that possible?

Outside, there were blue skies, and the day promised to be another scorcher. A trip to the outhouse was unavoidable, but this time we took Elizabeth along with us. Peering inside the outhouse's rickety door, we could clearly see the ants' nest inside, stacked up by one of the wooden walls.

"When they sensed Sierra, they swarmed," Elizabeth said grimly. "We'll buy some spray later. For now, I'm going to have to burn them."

As soon as she stepped inside the outhouse, the ants surged toward her, erupting from the nest in waves. She sprayed lighter fluid on them and then dropped a match on the wet clumps, jumping back as flames leapt toward the roof of the outhouse. Looking inside, I cringed when I saw roaches—giant forest roaches—squeeze out of hidden cracks and run along the inner walls, trying to escape the heat. Were we really going to have to use this shack for the next six weeks?

Later, Elizabeth took us down the road to a little store called Taylor's, and we bought milk, eggs, groceries, the strongest bug spray we could find, and four enamel chamber pots that we could use in the privacy of our bedrooms and empty into the outhouse. At least I could minimize having to actually sit down in that bug-infested shed!

Sierra's legs were red, swollen, and painful, but she came with us because she wanted to call her parents. The scratched pay phone near the old-style cash register was now our lifeline to the rest of the world.

Mrs. Taylor, the owner of the store, knew Elizabeth from previous field trips. "So you're back again, collecting songs?" she asked.

"Yes, this time I'm looking for songs about Big Jack. Have you ever heard any about him?"

An expression crossed Mrs. Taylor's face, as though she recognized the name, but she quickly replied, "No, I never heard of any Big Jack."

"Well, okay," Elizabeth said pleasantly. "If you ever hear someone mention him, can you let me know?" I noticed that Mrs. Taylor didn't answer.

I called home and let my parents know that for the next six weeks all the communication would be one-way, depending on when I could get to a phone.

"What if there's an emergency?" my mother asked. I had already wondered about the same thing.

"We won't even know where to find you!"

"It'll be okay, Mom," I reassured her, pretending to be more confident than I truly felt. She was right. Without my phone, I was completely out of touch with the outside world. And here on St. Pierre, no one knew me outside of the research team. That meant I was completely dependent on Elizabeth. To be honest, how well did I know her? She was just a professor I'd met earlier in the year.

It wasn't a good situation to be in, but I'd have to make the best of it. *At least you're not alone,* I told myself.

When we returned to the cottage, Caesar Cummings was standing in the sandy driveway like a silent sentinel. With a quiet snort of laughter, I wondered if he'd been there all night.

He watched as we got out of the car, holding himself stiffly, and then politely said, "G-Good morning."

"Good morning, Mr. Cummings," Elizabeth said cheerfully, "How are you this morning?"

"G-Good m-morning," Caesar repeated. I wondered about his mental state. "Did you sleep well, Miss Elizabeth?" he asked.

"Yes, we were fine, but the fire ants in the outhouse attacked Sierra. I need you to help me find their nests so that we can spray them." He didn't respond, but his cloudy eyes glanced toward the back yard.

"Oh, by the way," Elizabeth added, "we're interested in songs about Big Jack. Do you know any?" She was serious about asking everyone about the song.

"B-big J-J-Jack? I never heard anything about him," Caesar responded quickly. Why did I have a feeling that he was lying? He glanced again toward the back of the house. "I d-don't know anything about B-Big J-Jack," he repeated, and walked toward the fire ant nest in the back.

A little later, I was standing outside the cottage picking flowers in an effort to make my room feel more like home. A movement caught my attention, and looking up I saw Caesar silently watching me.

"Oh, hello, Mr. Cummings! You startled me."

He looked straight ahead, not at me, and said, almost to himself, "Stay away from B-Big J-Jack."

"What did you say?" I asked him. But he was walking away. "What did you say?" I repeated, running to catch up with him.

He looked toward me, smiled politely, and said, "G-Good day, M-Miss Finch. B-Be careful at n-night." Then he stepped into an ancient car that was parked near the gray cottage and drove away, churning up little drifts of sand.

17

Finch

May 21

In the afternoon, our research started in earnest. Elizabeth drove down shadowed roads with occasional houses and silent pedestrians, always, it seemed, searching for roads that were even more deserted. The grassy marshes and moss-laden trees pressed in on us from all sides. Occasionally a brilliantly white egret passed overhead, bent on some mission. With the terrors of the night before behind me, I could really appreciate the beauty of the island.

Eventually, Elizabeth stopped the car on a remote sandy road. It looked deserted, and we looked at her questioningly.

"This is where we'll start our research," she said. Where? I saw no one and no houses.

"Where are the people?" Russell asked, echoing my thoughts.

"They're down this road, which leads into a tomato plantation. Come on, we'll walk down there together and then divide up."

Down the road we dutifully trudged. The hot sand sifted into my sandals, and it was hard to walk. I kept having to stop. When we finally came to a little settlement of sun-bleached wooden houses lifted up on cement blocks, Elizabeth told us to divide up. She said we should walk up to the front porch, introduce ourselves, and explain that we were students visiting the island.

"Don't ask about Big Jack yet; just make a connection."

As I approached the first house she'd assigned to me, I saw children sitting on the porch watching me with blank expressions. Abruptly, two dogs rushed from beneath the house, teeth gleaming and barking furiously. I stopped in my tracks, terrified and wondering if their bites were going to end my research career. Fortunately, the dogs stopped at the edge of the yard, still barking wildly. I looked again at the children, who stared mutely back at me—and I retreated back to the sandy road.

One of the silent pedestrians passed in front of the house as I left. It was a man as old as Caesar Cummings, wearing a battered straw hat and overalls. He looked neither right nor left, and his movements had a peculiar gliding quality. To my surprise, when the dogs saw him they ran back under the house, and the children screamed and ran inside.

What the hell? St. Pierre was truly a strange, unfriendly place!

18

Finch

May 21

"Let's check out one of the local clubs," Elizabeth suggested after dinner. We'd eaten on the back porch, with a rusty fan pushing the hot air past our faces. It was slightly more pleasant than inside the stifling cottage.

"This'll give you a chance to get to know the local people better… and maybe they'll have air conditioning too."

"Speaking of maybe—maybe I'll get lucky," Russell said with a wink.

Sierra rolled her eyes and mumbled under her breath—and I wondered if any of the local men would notice me if they had her to look at. I was curvy and a lovely cinnamon brown—not at all bad looking, if you asked me. But Sierra had warm, honey-colored skin that was eye catching, especially in a place like St. Pierre where most of the people were a deeper chocolate brown.

The club was down one of St. Pierre's numerous sandy roads that didn't seem to lead anywhere in particular until you arrived at your destination. The parking area was almost full by the time we arrived, with cars parked this way and that under the trees close to a simple, one-story painted cement building adorned with a red neon sign that read "Sally's Club." Couples and small groups picked their way through the grass toward the entrance door. The place wasn't much to look at, but I could hear snatches of rhythm and blues every time the door opened. I recognized an old classic, "Stormy Monday," and smiled. Sally's Club might be all right.

Inside, several small tables circled a miniature dance floor, and we found one with four empty seats. At the tiny bandstand, a blues band was hard at work. The music and the vibe were tight. It was hot—despite the overworked window air conditioners—intense, and nothing like anything I'd ever experienced. I felt myself relaxing. St. Pierre might be strange in some ways, but the music was working its magic on me. All I needed now was a drink.

Russell volunteered to find the bar, which gave me a chance to check out the surroundings better. Everything, including the bandstand, bar, and a small kitchen area, was jammed into a single room. Musicians' photographs were the sole decoration on the walls. The air was thick with music, conversation, sweat, and the smells of food and drink. It was what my grandfather would have called a real *fonk*.

After only one day on the island, I didn't expect to see anyone I recognized, but pretty quickly I noticed a man sitting on the other side of the crowded room who was studying our group intently. When our eyes met, he gave a little nod. A few minutes later, he rose and, to my surprise, came over to our table. He was about Elizabeth's age, tall and thin, with dark-brown skin, bright eyes, and distinctive angular features. Despite the club's heat, he wore a closely cut dark suit with the jacket buttoned.

Elizabeth looked up as the man approached, and an expression I couldn't read passed briefly across her face. Then she stood as he said in a cool but friendly way, "Hello again, Elizabeth."

"Hello, Sam," she said a little stiffly, taking his extended hand.

"Why don't you introduce me to your friends?" he asked, with a restrained smile that didn't quite reach his eyes.

"Of course," she said, turning toward us. "Russell, Sierra, Finch, I'd like to introduce you to Sam Dent." We shook his hand in turns, leaning across the table.

"This is my research team," Elizabeth added with a tight smile.

"Pleased to meet you," Sam replied smoothly.

I couldn't read Elizabeth's relationship with Sam. They clearly knew each other from her previous trips, but she didn't seem entirely comfortable around him. Something about him seemed different from the other islanders we'd met so far. While I was thinking this over, I felt a tap on my shoulder and looked up to see one of the local men smiling and gesturing toward the center of the room.

Why not? I took the hand he offered, and we jostled our way through the other couples to a spot on the dance floor. My new partner was about my height and had a pleasant round face and sleepy eyes. He leaned in and asked, "What's your name?"

"Finch. What's yours?"

"I'm Andre. I never saw you around here before..."

"No, I just came here with Elizabeth." I gestured over his shoulder. "I'm here with her and with Russell and Sierra."

I looked toward the table and caught Russell whispering in Sierra's ear, with his hand on her arm. Her eyes were lowered, and she was smiling slightly. Feeling like I'd interrupted something, I looked back at Andre, smiled, and added, "We're students from Chicago. We're, uh, doing research here on folk songs with our professor, Elizabeth Wood."

"Oh yeah, I've seen her before," he responded, looking over at Elizabeth. "She goes around asking questions about old-time songs and rhymes. My granny talked to her once. She and Sam Dent are friends." *Really? They hardly acted like it.* "I've seen them walking around the marshes together in big rubber boots, like they was looking for something. But, you know, Sam's a little strange like that."

I was curious about what he meant but didn't ask about it just then. I liked the band, whose lead singer reminded me of Anthony Hamilton, and Andre and I moved well together. We danced to two fast numbers and shifted to a slower mode when the band began a bluesy number. Gradually, I lost track of time. The whole room seemed to exhale heat and sexuality. My blouse clung to my back, and my forehead was damp with perspiration.

Andre grasped my waist and moved in closer. I took advantage of his nearness to ask, "How is Sam strange?"

This wasn't the question he expected, I'm sure. "He—" he began, but cut his answer short when he saw Russell walking toward us.

"Excuse me, brother," Russell said to Andre, moving smoothly between the two of us. "I'd like to have this dance. By the way, there's a lonely lady sitting over there"—he pointed with his head at Sierra—"if you need a partner."

Russell stepped in close and grabbed me around my damp lower back. Taking advantage of the press of the other couples, he held me tightly, and we moved slowly to the pulsing rhythm of the music.

A full-figured woman squeezed into a blue sparkly dress sang, "Daddy, your lovin' sure is good," as she hugged the mike.

"Umm..." Russell said in my ear, "I could get to like it here."

I smiled without responding, and we danced through that song and the next one, sung by a husky older man.

> *Big fat mama don't mean me no good;*
> *Now, she's a big fat mama, don't mean me no good;*
> *Now, just pack your things, and move to the Piney Wood*
> *Don't tell no story, don't tell me no lie;*
> *Don't tell no story, don't tell me no lie;*
> *Now, you's a good looking mama, but you was born to die*
> *I'm gonna sprinkle a little goofer dust all around your nappy*
> *   head;*
> *I'm gonna sprinkle a little goofer dust all around your head;*
> *You wake up some of these mornings and find your own self*
> *   dead*
> *Now, if you don't like me, mama, don't keep on teasing me;*
> *Now, if you don't like me, mama, don't keep on teasing me;*
> *'Cause I can find somebody else that will give me sympathy*
> *I'm gonna leave you, mama, 'cause you will not do;*
> *I'm gonna leave you, mama, 'cause you will not do;*
> *Lord, I got another fat mama, and I don't want you.*

I recognized an old blues song called "Big Fat Mamma Blues" and shivered at the reference to goofer dust. Did the people on St. Pierre believe that some magic dust could kill someone?

Russell felt my shiver and hugged me closer. I pulled back a little, and he laughed softly. "Come on, Finch, don't you like me?"

"I barely know you," I said sarcastically and pulled away from our sweaty embrace. "And anyway, I'm burning up. I need some air."

I pushed myself past the other dancers and walked to the door. It was a hot and humid night, but still cooler outside than in the club. A slight breeze began drying the sweat on my face, and I held my blouse out to get some air against my skin.

I was so involved in cooling down that at first I didn't notice there were other people outdoors. As my eyes grew accustomed to the dark, I saw their silhouetted bodies under the trees. Some were couples or small groups talking quietly, while others were couples embracing.

And then I saw them: Sam and Elizabeth in a tight caress, the back of his head bent over her face and his thin body pressing hers firmly against the gritty concrete wall. *Andre was right about them being friends—and a little more than that.*

Not knowing if they'd seen me, I turned and fled back inside the dense heat of Sally's Club. Russell and Sierra were dancing now, and I sat at the table alone, watching them. Was Russell also asking her if she liked him?

A few minutes later, Elizabeth came in by herself, smoothing her rumpled clothes as she walked. She sat down and gave me a quick smile.

"Finch, dear, it's so hot in here. Can you get me another drink?"

"Of course," I answered, hoping that my face didn't give my thoughts away.

19

Elizabeth
May 21

Saturday night at Sally's was my first time seeing Sam since we arrived on St. Pierre. I thought I might find him there; it was kind of our hangout from the summer before. When the kids got up to dance, he leaned over, squeezed my arm, and said in a purring voice, "Elizabeth, I've missed you. You're as beautiful as ever."

"Mmm," I said, looking into his intense, inky eyes. "You can flatter me any day, Mr. Dent." We laughed together. Then I turned more serious. "Why did you ask me to bring a team with me? What did you find out?"

He put a finger to my lips, and said, "Sh-h-h. So many questions. All things will become known in time."

His touch was electric, and he knew it. I didn't like how he used our mutual attraction to avoid answering my questions, but to be honest there was something about him that I couldn't resist. It was sexual…but more than that; it was almost like he had put a spell on me.

"Are you sure you haven't worked some roots on me?" I asked him only half-jokingly.

He stood up and took my hand. "Come on, let's go outside where we can get some air."

Outside, it was indeed cooler. There was a nearly half moon, and the trees shivered in a slight breeze. We stood away from other couples and talked over our plans. Sam said, "I've gone through a lot of old historical records, and I'm pretty sure I've located the site of Big Jack's cabin. The problem we had before was that we didn't know the name of the plantation he lived on, but I've been looking at deeds in the courthouse, and I think I'm on the right track. A few weeks from now will be a good time to check it out, because the moon will be full."

"Why are we going at night?" I asked. "Won't it be easier to do this during the day?"

He leaned toward me and said softly, "Do you want everyone to see us? I think we'll do better with privacy." He nuzzled my ear, and I pushed him away…but not too hard.

"And you still haven't told me why you wanted me to bring the kids. Why can't you and I do this ourselves?" Instead of answering, he leaned in with his full body this time and gave me a slow, deep kiss, seductively pressing his erection against me and digging my back into Sally's rough concrete wall.

20

Finch
May 22

In the early days of our research, we had a routine—until everything changed forever. In those early days, we divided up every day to talk *or try to talk* to people about "old-time songs" they might know. On bad days, I ran from a lot of dogs. On good days, people invited me onto their porches and asked who I was and what had brought me to St. Pierre. If they were older, they were more likely to know a few songs and stories, but it could be hard to understand their Gullah accents. It was easier to talk with the kids, but they couldn't tell us anything we wanted to know.

In general, it was frustrating, because so few people said they knew anything about Big Jack. On many days we came back to the house hot, dusty, and no farther along than where we'd started out in the morning.

That never seemed to discourage Elizabeth. "It's the nature of fieldwork," she'd say with annoying cheerfulness. "We just have to stay at it until we find the right person."

I didn't see much of Caesar Cummings, and I wondered what he was up to when he wasn't at his little gray house next door.

One day, when I was walking down one of the roads near our house, I came upon an elderly woman who was sitting outside her small cottage with a bowl of snap peas in her lap. She invited me to sit down with her and introduced herself as Miss Myma. I could tell that she was one of the oldest women on the island. Her back was bent from years of hard work in the fields, but her eyes were still warm and bright. She wore her hair in neat braids with twists of white cloth at the end.

We liked each other immediately, and she offered to take me fishing. We went the next day, leaving early before the heat of the day had set in, carrying nets, buckets, and short, blunt sticks. "Is this a fishing pole?" I asked her, gesturing with mine, and she laughed.

"You ever go fishing before?"

"No ma'am."

She laughed again and said, "You'll see what the sticks are for." I hoped we wouldn't be beating the fish to death with them, but I kept that thought to myself.

We walked down the road to a sandy path that took us to the edge of one of the salt creeks. It was a radiantly clear day, and the sun reflecting from the water was almost blinding. The salty smell that had seemed so strange at first now struck me as familiar and pleasant. It was an intimate part of this powerful and distinctive environment.

Myma took off her shoes, hitched her skirts up around her waist, and waded into the water. I followed behind her, feeling the warm mud oozing between my toes. We walked carefully, avoiding outcroppings of oysters, until we were about knee deep in the sluggish, muddy water. Then we waited. I wasn't sure what was going to happen next until Myma quickly dipped her net into the water and brought it back up with a twisting, silvery fish inside.

The fish's desperate death throes were the closest I'd ever been to the immediacy of life and death, and I unexpectedly felt personally responsible for taking its life. I quietly vowed that I'd make sure we didn't waste a single bite of it, as I uncomfortably mediated on how different this was from the sanitized experience of buying a piece of fish at the store—or fish sticks, for that matter, which didn't even resemble the animal they'd once been.

"Now you catch one," Myma said.

"What?" Somehow, I'd thought I could just be an observer.

"Now you catch a fish. Just watch the water and plunge the net in like I did."

It was easier said than done. After several unsuccessful tries, my bucket was empty, the sun was high and hot, and mosquitoes were swarming irritatingly around my face. "Why aren't the mosquitoes bothering you, Miss Myma?" I asked, and in response she pulled a handful of herbs from her pocket.

"Rub these on your arms and legs," she said. "They will chase them away."

The herbs had a peculiar sharp smell that seemed to work. Myma was the first person I'd met who knew about plants, and I wanted to ask her about that. But first, I was determined to show her that I could catch fish too.

I felt the water stir near one of my legs and saw the shifting shape of a good-sized fish, tantalizingly close. With determination, I waited until what felt like the right moment, and then I quickly dipped my net beneath it.

This time, I knew I'd been successful, feeling the heavy, squirming weight of the fish in my net. I dumped it into the bucket, where, heaving and tossing, it joined the ones Myma had caught, its scales gleaming in the sun. Again, I felt the weight of responsibility for taking a life, and thought that my relationship to meat would never be quite the same again.

After I surprised myself by catching another fish, Myma and I stopped for lunch, sitting on the grass by the side of the creek to eat sandwiches. She asked me where I had met Elizabeth, and I explained that I was one of her students at the university.

"Is a university like a school?"

"Yes, it's the school you can go to after high school." Because the local school system was so limited, I'd had to explain this to several people.

"I went only to third grade," she said simply," even though I wanted to go higher."

"What happened?"

"The white man whose farm my father worked on wanted my sister and me to help in the field. My father said no, but the white man came to school one day and took us out of class."

"What? Couldn't you go back?"

"No, the white man said he would make my father leave St. Pierre unless we kept working on his farm. So we never went back to school."

She said it simply and unemotionally, as though that was the way of the world—which it had been for her. In fact, I'd already learned that back when Myma was young education on St. Pierre for Black children was limited to elementary school. Many local people her age had never gone past sixth grade because there was no bus to the secondary schools on a neighboring island. Complicating matters was the unchallenged power of local white landowners, who could use people however they liked.

Inwardly, I seethed. Her story was not what my parents—or even my grandparents—had ever experienced, but if they had lived in the South, it could have been their story too.

"Are you ready to catch some crabs?" Myma asked, breaking into my thoughts.

"I guess so. Do we use the nets again?"

"No, we use the sticks now. But first we have to walk to where they live."

We waded down the creek to where the water was shallow and rimmed by a broad muddy bank. As we approached, several large crabs darted sideways into holes that led beneath the mud.

Myma handed me one of the sticks and then stood near one of the holes. She motioned to me to do the same, and I dutifully took my position.

"What?" I started to ask.

"Sh-h-h."

For several minutes, nothing happened. Then, a large crab cautiously emerged from its hole and began scuttling across the mud. Within seconds, Myma had pinned it across the back with her stick.

She lifted it carefully, avoiding the pincers, and dropped it into one of our buckets.

"Now you try," she said, smiling encouragingly.

I laughed. "I don't think so!"

As the hot afternoon wore on, Myma caught three more crabs, and I caught...none. They were too fast for me, and I was too hesitant. By the time I'd made up my mind to move, they were invariably back in their holes. I was relieved when she said it was time for us to return home.

As I walked back with Myma after a day enjoying nature at its fullest, St. Pierre seemed momentarily like the perfect place to be. But then Myma broke the spell, asking, "Do you know how to tell a ghost when you a-see one?"

"What? A ghost?" I said, startled. *She talked about ghosts as though they were real.*

"Yes, darling. There are ghosts walking up and down the road; all the time they walk up and down the road." I felt my spine go cold. "How you know them is that they don't have no feet. If you see a person without feet, then you know it's a ghost. And they have a funny way of moving, a kind of gliding way of moving."

I thought of the man in the straw hat whom I'd passed on the sandy road, and the way the children and dogs had run from him. But maybe it was just an old superstition. There was probably a perfectly good explanation. Still, her absolute certainty made me uncomfortable.

"What should I do if I see a ghost?" I asked, just to see what she would say.

"Don't speak to it!" she said firmly. "Just keep walking."

The topic made me nervous, so, changing the subject, I asked, "Miss Myma, have you ever heard a song about someone named Big Jack?"

She looked at me sharply. "No need to ask about Big Jack," she said. It was a warning, like Caesar's. And she fingered something at her neck. I saw it was an amulet like the one he wore.

"Is there something wrong with Big Jack?" I asked.

"I don't even like to say his name," she said. We walked the rest of the way back to her house in silence.

When I told Elizabeth what Myma had said about Big Jack, she just waved her hand and said, "I told you that some of these people are superstitious. They don't like the Big Jack song because of the way he died. That's all. Now let's fry up some of those fish you caught."

21

Finch

May 25

I was finishing up a call on the pay phone when Mrs. Taylor looked up from the register and said shyly that a woman called Miss Kat ("with a K") might know something about Big Jack. It was the first time she had volunteered any information related to our research, and this was an encouraging development.

"That's good news," I said with genuine enthusiasm. "Where can I find her?"

"Go down Sandy Point Road about half a mile and look for the old house on the right-hand side." She looked down quickly, like a crab retreating into its shell.

Sandy Point Road was in walking distance, and I started out after lunch, walking on the edge of the road and avoiding the treacherous underbrush with its aggressive bugs and poisonous snakes. Trudging down the quiet roads was relaxing, but people's repeated warnings about natural and supernatural hazards kept me constantly vigilant.

The road was in exceptionally poor condition, and my walk was slow going. I passed several houses, hustled past a few growling dogs, and after about half a mile began looking for Miss Kat's house. Since many of the houses fit the description, I wasn't sure what would distinguish hers.

The next house I came to looked deserted. A short, unsteady flight of broken front stairs led to an unpainted frame building with a partially caved-in roof. Chickens walked freely in and out of the splintered doorway. *This can't be the one I'm looking for,* I thought and kept walking.

After walking for another fifteen minutes, I was forced to conclude that I'd passed the house I was looking for. Grassy marshes stretched on either side of the road, with no sign of any buildings on the horizon. In the distance, I saw a wooden dock that probably marked the "sandy point" the road eventually led to.

I heard a whispering sound behind me and spun around. Nothing. Just strands of hanging moss that shifted softly in the breeze. Wait— did I see someone walking into the bushes by the side of the road? Who would do that, knowing that cottonmouths and rattlesnakes lurked in the grass? I shivered and noticed that the wind was picking up. It was time to retrace my steps before I got caught in one of St. Pierre's notoriously fierce afternoon storms.

I walked back to the vicinity of the ramshackle house with the chickens and looked around carefully for signs of any other dwellings. Across the road from the old house, a battered mobile home occupied a sandy lot, elevated on cinder blocks. It was the wrong side of the road according to my directions from Mrs. Taylor, but maybe she'd been mistaken or I'd misheard her.

I walked slowly into the yard, keeping an eye out for charging dogs, but the coast was clear. I peered through the mobile home's partially open screen door at a jumbled kitchen and knocked. No answer. I knocked again, and called, "Miss Kat? Miss Kat, are you home?"

I was turning back down the path, discouraged, when I heard the door open behind me. "You lookin' for Miss Kat?" a woman's voice asked.

"Yes!" I said enthusiastically, grateful for the human contact. I turned and saw a young woman about my age, dressed casually in a cotton blouse and pants. "I'm one of the students who's with Elizabeth

Wood," I quickly explained. "We're doing research on the song about Big Jack, and Mrs. Taylor at the store said Miss Kat might be able to help me."

"I know who you are," she said neutrally. "You and those other two are going around asking about old-time stuff."

"Yeah. It's kind of interesting. Do people our age"—I met her eyes briefly—"care about those old songs and stories?"

"I heard about them when I was young. We all do."

"Do you believe all that stuff about ghosts?"

"Do you?" she countered. "Isn't that what you want to ask my grandmother about?"

"Well not about ghosts, exactly. I want to ask your grandmother—uh, Miss Kat—about Big Jack. Do you mean that Miss Kat is your grandmother?"

I felt flustered. Meanwhile, she looked at me like I was stupid and didn't respond. Belatedly, I remembered that on St. Pierre people tended to live in family clusters.

"Do you know where I can find Miss Kat?" I asked, hoping she'd answer that she was resting inside the trailer.

"She stays over there," she answered, pointing at the broken-down house across the road.

You've got to be kidding, I thought, hoping this didn't show on my face. "Oh, okay. I'll check over there for her."

The woman glanced at the house and said flatly, "Mama's not there now. Try again tomorrow." She saw my puzzled look and added, "She's my grandmother, but I call her Mama because she raised me."

"Okay," I repeated. "Thanks for your help. My name is Finch. Can you tell her I was looking for her?"

"I'm Cheryl," she said, offering her hand. "I'm leaving here soon," she added.

I was confused. "Do you mean you're leaving to go to the store or something?" I didn't see a car in the yard, and there weren't any stores that I knew of in walking distance.

"No, I'm leaving St. Pierre. Where do you live?" she asked abruptly.

"Me? I'm from Chicago."

"Where is that? Is it up north?"

It never ceased to amaze me—St. Pierre was so insular that some young people had never been any farther than Charleston. It wasn't such a surprise with the older generation, but people my age? Yes, them too. "Uh, yeah. It's a big city about a thirteen-hour drive from here. You can make it in a day if you start really early."

"They have good jobs there? I'm looking for work."

"You can get work if you have skills. What kinds of things can you do?"

"I had a job in Charleston for a while cleaning a white lady's house. And I can take care of kids. Do they have those kinds of jobs in Chicago?"

I sighed inwardly. St. Pierre had beautiful scenery and the heritage of a vibrant folk culture, but after centuries of slavery followed by years of Jim Crow segregation, it was also depressingly poor and underdeveloped. There was very little work for young people like Cheryl other than working in someone's house or in the fields. Economically, not much had changed in hundreds of years.

An alternative occurred to me. "Have you ever thought of the military? I don't know much about it, but I know it's a way to get job training, and they're always looking for volunteers."

Cheryl nodded. "That's something to think about. I have a friend who did that." I heard footsteps, and a little girl about four years old appeared in the trailer door. She was disheveled, like she'd just gotten up from a nap. "Mama, I'm hungry," she complained. "I want to eat." Cheryl waved and turned to go. I wished I could do something to help her. We were about the same age, but the paths of our lives were so different.

Painfully aware of how sheltered I was from the reality of life for Cheryl and most of the people on St. Pierre, I headed back for our house, planning to return another day to visit Miss Kat.

22

Finch
May 26

When I returned the next day, the door to Cheryl's mobile home was tightly closed, and there were no signs of life in the yard. I had hoped she could introduce me to her grandmother, but now I was on my own.

The yard in front of Miss Kat's house was hard dirt, spotted white with the chickens' droppings. I climbed the short, decayed entry stairs, stepping carefully to avoid the caved-in portions and shooing away two chickens that stood at the top. I knocked on the half-open door, and it shifted open slightly. I peered cautiously into the musty, dark interior.

"Miss Kat," I called. I heard clucking inside the house, but no answering voice. "Miss Kat," I called again. "My name is Finch. I talked to Cheryl yesterday, and I've come to see you today."

I thought I heard a muffled response, so I pushed the door open and entered the front room. It was in terrible condition, with a hole in the ceiling that was open to the distant, hot sky and slanting, rotted floorboards. How could anyone live here? Part of me wanted to run away as fast as I could.

Faintly, a woman's voice said, "I'm in here," and I walked toward the sound, stepping carefully. The front room led directly to a dimly lit bedroom, where a thin woman lay in an old iron bed, propped up on a discolored pillow.

"Miss Kat?" I asked. The woman stared at me with cloudy eyes and nodded. She seemed very old, with a lined brown face and wispy hair covered by a dirty white head rag.

"My name is Finch," I repeated, perching on a battered wooden stool that was next to the bed. "How are you today?"

She made an indifferent motion with her mouth and yawned, still staring. Something told me that she'd been drinking. I felt something brush my ankle and jumped off the stool. But it was just one of the chickens that had followed me into the bedroom. The indignity and squalor of the woman's poverty were almost too much for me to bear, but I made myself focus. I wasn't sure what she could tell me about Big Jack, but I was determined to try to find out.

I pushed the chicken away with my foot and sat back down. "Miss Kat, can I ask you a question?" Her head shifted restlessly, and she mumbled something like "yes."

"I'm here with Elizabeth Wood, the professor from Chicago. Have you heard of her?"

Miss Kat shifted her feet and said thickly, "Yes, I hear about her."

"I'm a student at the university where Miss Kat teaches." No response. "We're interested in the, uh, songs and stories that you have here on St. Pierre."

Now, to my surprise, she chuckled, and said, "Old-time people, them tell plenty stories; not so much now."

"I know," I agreed. "That's why we're here. Elizabeth wants to collect as many songs and stories as she can, before people forget about them."

Miss Kat reached under the bed's soiled top sheet and extracted a small, unlabeled bottle that contained a brown liquid. She took a quick swig. I wanted to take the bottle from her, but of course I didn't. I just watched helplessly, thinking that I'd better ask her about Big Jack before she was too far gone to answer.

"Miss Kat, have you heard of a song about a man called Big Jack?"

A nervous look flickered across her face, and her dull eyes focused sharply on me for a moment. "Big Jack? Long time since I hear of him."

"But have you heard of him before? Do you remember what you heard?"

She closed her eyes and pressed her lips together. Just when I'd decided she'd fallen asleep, she reached under the covers again and took another swig from her flask. I figured she was drinking some of the local bootleg liquor, and I was quietly amazed it hadn't killed her yet. She was fragilely thin, and I wondered how often she ate. I desperately hoped her granddaughter Cheryl would find a way to leave St. Pierre, but what would happen to Miss Kat when she did?

Miss Kat turned her face away from me and said something under her breath. I thought I heard the words "Big Jack."

"I'm sorry," I said. "I missed that. Did you say something?"

"Big Jack brook."

"Big Jack brook?"

"Ummm," she responded, pushing her face into the pillow.

"Are you saying 'Big Jack brook,' Miss Kat, like Big Jack lived by a brook?"

"Big Jack lived on St. Pierre."

"Right, he lived on St. Pierre. Did he live by a brook?" They didn't usually call the creeks "brooks" in St. Pierre, but it was possible the song used that word.

"No," she said impatiently, "Big Jack lived by water." I felt like we were going in circles.

"So what about the brook?" I asked again. She turned her head and stared at me without responding. Then her eyes gradually closed, and she fell asleep.

I left, picking my way past the chickens and pulling the outside door closed behind me. It was still quiet at Cheryl's trailer. That was unfortunate, because I could have used her moral support.

23

Finch
June 2

What could "Big Jack brook" mean?

I could have gone back to Miss Kat's house to ask her again, but I didn't have the heart for it. Not yet. Her house was so wretched, and she was so far from my mental image of how someone's grandmother should live that I just couldn't face seeing her again so soon. I decided to talk to some other people first.

Over the next days, Russell, Sierra, and I went in and out of houses and yards. Repeatedly, we asked, "Have you heard of Big Jack? Do you know anything about Big Jack's song?" We noticed that when we asked about Big Jack people sometimes gave a quick look around as though they were afraid of being overheard. That was spooky.

One white-haired man I talked to while he was digging in his garden told me that Big Jack was a tall, strong man who had worked on the railroad. He said that Big Jack died trying to outrace a steam drill. I dutifully wrote that down, even though privately I thought he'd confused Big Jack with John Henry, the "steel-driving" man who "hammered so hard that he broke his po' heart / And he laid down his hammer and he died."

Another elderly man told Sierra that he'd heard when he was a boy that Big Jack was a pirate who raided the coastal plantations and hid his spoils among the salt marshes. This was exciting news at our evening meeting, because it meant we could be on the right track for uncovering a song about Big Jack's treasure. I looked over at Elizabeth, expecting her to share our excitement, but instead her expression was strangely blank.

"Aren't you pleased?" I asked her. "We've only been here a short while and already we're on the trail of Big Jack's treasure." She gave a kind of forced smile and said, "Don't mind me; I'm just tired. I agree, you're off to a great start."

By the end of our first two weeks on St. Pierre, we had identified two verses that people consistently said were the beginning of Big Jack's song. Oddly, there was a major difference in them from the story Elizabeth had told us on our first night. For, as it turned out, only one person—the elderly man Sierra talked to—associated Big Jack with a hidden treasure. What we heard more often was that he had a book.

The verses went:

> Big Jack had a secret book
> *He did; yes, he did*
> He kept it by his side
> *He did; yes, he did*
> He lived beside the water
> *He did; yes, he did*
> Where the salt marsh meets the tide
> *He did; yes, he did.*

"Why does the song talk about a book, Elizabeth?" Russell asked. "You told us that Big Jack took the massa's treasure."

To my surprise, a look I can only call *shifty* crossed her face.

"It's unexpected for sure," she replied quickly, almost guiltily. "If slaves weren't allowed to read, it would be unusual for them to have books. But these old songs change over the years, so maybe a line about treasure turned into one about a book. Let's just keep asking questions and see what we can find out." She smiled at Russell, but it looked forced, as though she had something else on her mind.

For me, the lines about the book explained what Miss Kat had been trying to say. I was certain that what I'd heard as "Big Jack brook" was actually "Big Jack book." I decided I'd go back to ask her more questions. Maybe I could catch her on a good day when she hadn't been drinking.

24

Finch

June 6

Walking toward Miss Kat's house, I noticed that the outer door of Cheryl's trailer was open, so I stopped there first. I rapped on the screen, and Cheryl's daughter ran to answer, peering through the mesh. "Mama!" she shouted. "That lady's at the door!"

"Cheryl, it's me, Finch," I called out. She answered the door, drying her hands on a dishcloth, and invited me in. Unlike her mother's house, Cheryl's trailer was neatly kept, but it was almost unbearably hot and stuffy. Even with the outer door open, not much air got through the screen door. Cheryl waved me to a well-worn couch, where a cat curled among the cushions, and joined me there a few minutes later, bringing two glasses of sweet iced tea from the kitchen. Meanwhile, her daughter brought a doll and began playing at our feet.

"Did you get to talk to Mama?" Cheryl asked conversationally.

"I did...a little. I visited her the day after that time I talked to you. I think she was kind of tired."

"Yeah, she gets tired a lot these days," Cheryl said sarcastically, barking a short laugh.

"But she gave me a clue." I wanted to avoid the topic of Miss Kat's condition.

"Say what? She knew something about this song you guys are going around asking about?"

"Yeah, she kept saying 'Big Jack brook,' and I thought she was talking about water. But it turns out she was saying 'Big Jack book.' That's what we have found out so far from our research. Big Jack's song is about a book he had."

"Really? A slave with a book? Was that allowed? No wonder the old folks made a song about it. What was in Big Jack's book?"

"We don't know yet; that's the next thing we have to find out."

"Are you going to ask Mama about it?"

"I thought I would try."

"You'd better catch her now before she gets started," Cheryl said wryly. Even though I hadn't responded to her earlier comment, I appreciated her frankness about Miss Kat. In my own family, people preferred to ignore unpleasant facts.

The chickens were in Miss Kat's yard as usual. Now, some scrawny chicks that chirped and scratched the dirt in imitation of their elders joined the big ones. Sighing quietly, I climbed the sagging, broken steps and entered the dark interior of the house. The only light was a shaft of sun that pierced the dusty air through the hole in the ceiling of the front room. The light pinpointed thin swirls of dust that swayed in the air like ghostly visitors.

"Miss Kat?" I called. "It's Finch."

"Back here," a cracked voice answered.

I followed the sound to the rear of the house, where Miss Kat stood on the rotted boards that constituted the back porch, pitching gray dishwater into the bushes. Standing, she appeared to be as fragile as her house, a tiny brown woman in a threadbare flowered dress that fell below her knees.

"Miss Kat, it's good to see you again," I said as cheerfully as I could muster.

"Have we met before?" She peered at me questioningly with her cloudy eyes. It was a sure bet that she'd never seen an eye doctor in her life.

"Yes, I came to see you a week or so ago. You seemed a little tired that day, but you were very helpful."

"Was I?" Leaning on a cane, she walked back into the house, and I followed. "What did I help you with?"

"We were talking about Big Jack." She glanced at me over her shoulder but didn't respond. "I'm here with Elizabeth Wood, and we're trying to find out if there's a song about Big Jack," I continued. "Do you remember that we were talking about that?"

"No," she said simply, walking into the bedroom.

I pressed on. "Well, you told me that you remembered 'Big Jack brook,' and I found out from talking to other people that Big Jack had a book. You were the first person to mention a book. Brook-book, brook-brook," I added, to illustrate the connection.

"That's nice," she said vaguely. She'd begun picking through piles of clothes that adorned the corners of the room and the stool where I'd sat on the previous visit.

I leaned on the stool and asked, "Do you want to hear a little bit of the song?" I hoped this would jog her memory and she could add another verse.

"Okay," she said without much enthusiasm. After two weeks of research, I'd gotten used to this kind of muted response. Maybe people didn't like being questioned, but it was also pretty clear to me that it had something to do with Big Jack.

I recited:

> Big Jack had a secret book
> *He did; yes, he did*
> He kept it by his side
> *He did; yes, he did*
> He lived beside the water
> *He did; yes, he did*
> Where the salt marsh meets the tide
> *He did; yes, he did.*

"Does that sound familiar?" I asked. Miss Kat stared at me, and in that brief second I knew that she *knew* something about Big Jack. But then she dropped her eyes and shook her head.

"No, I don't know that song. There's plenty of old-time songs that I don't know. You have to ask somebody else."

"But you knew that Big Jack had a book!" I protested. She shook her head again and sat on the bed with her back to me. The straw mattress crunched beneath her weight.

"I'm tired now…" she protested. She'd clearly forgotten my name. "Finch," I prompted. "I'm tired, Finch," she repeated. "I need to rest."

"Miss Kat, do you think you could remember the rest of the song if you thought about it?" I asked, persevering. "You know, maybe I could come back in a few days and you would remember more of it." I knew I was being a pest, but that look we'd exchanged told me that she knew more than she was saying.

"Stay away!" she said, suddenly and sharply. "Stay away!"

Rebuffed, I retreated down the rickety stairs. The startled chickens scattered hastily, raising little puffs of dust. Only later did I understand that what I'd taken for personal rejection was actually a warning.

25

Sam
June 9

The glistening light of an almost-full moon leads me into the grave-yard where my people sleep. I call them my army—they are the broken souls that live again through me. They were broken by bondage, suffering, and poverty, but when I gather them with me they are whole again.

They rise from the earth as I walk through the low mounds of ancient graves. Their forms are filmy and elusive at first, then gradually take shape. Their voices are soft, like the wind in the pines, then they too grow substantial. Sometimes my people sing and other times they moan and cry. It is all like music to me—music that is as old as time and captures the joy and sadness of being alive.

In the secret shadows of Mount Hombori in the African savannah, I learned how to summon my army. And because of my profound suffering there, I am forever bonded with them.

One by one, they join me under the trees. Their sad faces are contorted by what they have lived through, and their limbs are often twisted from pain and abuse, but they are beautiful to me. Here is George Anderson, who died when he was twenty-one. He has a scar on his neck below his left ear, three scars on his hands, and a scar on his forehead between his eyes. Melvina Beckly, a small child, has a shattered jaw from the dog that mauled her to death. Margaret, who never had a last name, is a teenager whose left ear is missing and whose right arm is scarred. Ellen Carter, in her midtwenties, is horribly burned on her face and arms.

Most of my people bear some visible mark from their life on the plantation, and of course they have internal wounds that don't show. But when we gather together, they forget their sorrows and celebrate their return to life.

Two of my favorites are Bina and Tolo. Bina was the wife of the legendary African they called Big Jack, and Tolo was his son. She is a tall, attractive woman whose left hand is missing several fingers. She was tortured after Big Jack died—enough to do harm but of course not enough to jeopardize her work in the fields—but she never revealed his secrets. She tells me she never knew them, but I'm not sure I believe her.

Sometimes Bina and I walk together, just the two of us, by the waterside, and I ask her gently about Big Jack's book. Sometimes we have sex, my body mounting hers and mingling ecstatically with her shadowy form, but even then she says nothing. I am patient, though. I have time on my side, and now I have Elizabeth's help. Elizabeth, who foolishly thinks I'm helping *her.*

Meanwhile, I'm cultivating Tolo, Big Jack's son. He's smart, like the father he never knew, and a natural leader. He grew up on St. Pierre, like me, and the spirit of the island is in him. He's my lieutenant; together, man and spirit, we rule my army.

Now that I have summoned my people, we travel to our secret place. Slipping a canoe into the creek, I cross the quiet water until I reach the island where Big Jack lived. My army follows behind me. If you saw them, you might think it was a mist traveling across the surface of the water. The locals know better though, and they avoid the graveyard and creeks at night.

I moor my canoe on the shores of the wild, unclaimed island where the remains of Big Jack's cabin still stand, protected by thickets of untamed underbrush. After Big Jack's death, and the devastation that followed it, people said his cabin was cursed, and no one went near it again. But unbeknownst to the whites—and many of the Blacks—some of the old believers created a secret gathering place beneath Big Jack's cabin where they could safely worship—a place where they could be free to dance, sing, and honor the gods of their homeland.

I follow an overgrown path to Big Jack's cabin, two small rooms with a deeply slanting roof and a single chimney. Made of oyster shells and clay, it seems to glow in the moonlight. I enter its shadowy interior and make my way to the back, where a wooden trapdoor is concealed in the dirt floor.

I descend through an old tunnel that has been carved into the subsoil of the island, feeling the cool air rise to meet me and breathing in the familiar earthy scent of the surrounding walls. My army fills the space behind me like a cloud, and we gradually go deeper, with just the soft tapping of dripping water as our accompaniment.

Eventually, the ground evens out and I am standing in a vast cave whose walls are covered, floor to ceiling, in painted symbols. They were profoundly meaningful to the Africans who drew them, but all of that is lost to the people living on St. Pierre today. Even Elizabeth, for all of her research, would have no idea of their significance if she saw them—which she won't.

For my army, and for me—because of my years of secret study—the symbols are powerfully meaningful. They make this cave a place of timeless joy and sacred connection. In times past, the drums that are the heart of African religion could be played here without detection. The slaves could sing, dance, and worship in peace, protected by the sheltering rocks.

My spirit army begins to manifest into semihuman form, and I am no longer alone. Bina, Tolo, George, Melvina, Margaret, Ellen, and the others all stand around me. The cave fills with the sound of drumming as the ceremony that unites me with my people begins.

My people's sensual African religion shocked puritanical Europeans, who were estranged from their own bodies and associated the flesh with sin. But my army and I understand that the vital force of the gods is present in everything that lives. Powered by the heartbeat of the drums, we channel that vital force through our dances and songs.

Two of the men carry enormous mortars into the center of the cave from the recesses where they've been hidden. Two more bring huge pestles and settle them into the mortars. On both, I draw symbols in white chalk that resemble the symbols on the wall. A woman hands me an armful of fruits and special roots, and I bless them, point them to the four corners of the cave, and then place them in the mortars. The men begin beating the pestles rhythmically, filling the air with the fragrance of the plants. The dance begins.

Soon, Bina is filled with the spirit of one of the gods. She gives a sharp cry, winds a red cloth around her shoulders, and pulls her dress up around her hips, exposing her muscular thighs. She leaps onto the lip of one of the giant mortars and dances there, her hands on her gyrating hips and her legs spread apart for balance. I admire her grace and strength as the men beat the pestles faster and faster and her dancing accelerates. Margaret jumps onto the edge of the second mortar. She too is filled with a god and shrieks with joy as her hips keep rhythm with the sweating drummers. As the dance grows faster and faster, some men hold the mortars down while the others drum furiously with the pestles.

Suddenly, Bina reaches up with her arms and rises into the air, still dancing. She cries out, and Margaret responds, their voices rising to the ceiling of the cave. The women are partly human and yet they are also gods. In them, the past and the present, the dead and the living, and the earthly and the unseen are mingled.

I am their lord, and you would no longer recognize me, for now my face is white, as white as a skull, and my features are those of a skeleton. Here in this cave, I can reveal my true self as Baron Samedi, the loa who rules the crossroads between the living and the dead. I was once just a man, but now I walk two worlds, and I have powers in both. Big Jack's book of secrets will make me even more powerful—if I can just get my hands on it.

At my signal, the drumming stops. The mortars are emptied, and more fruits and roots are blessed and added to them. The sweating, exultant dancers rest.

I signal again, and the drumming and dancing restart. This time, the gods fill several men and women. Their movements are sensual, but their expressions are almost remote, because they are communing with the gods.

One of the men lights a large fire near the center of the cave, and the air heats quickly, smelling intensely of the pounded fruits and the sweating bodies of the dancers. Some of them dance into the flames and out again, shouting with joy as they do so. They are bathed in the heat and light of the holy blaze, but do not burn. I spit rum into the flames to fan them higher and then dance into them myself, feeling their warm embrace of my hands, feet, and skeletal face. Fire, drums, dancers, gods—we are one. The drumming continues long into the night, and my people dance and sing for hours. They are alive and whole again, their anguished lives temporarily forgotten.

Eventually, our pace slows, as we sense that dawn is coming. The fire is extinguished, and the men return the mortars and pestles to their places. I remount the muddy path that leads to the surface and paddle my canoe back to the mainland. On the horizon, an orange line signals the sunrise, and the first birds are beginning to stir in the trees. Occasional ripples reveal the movement of large fish below the surface of the water.

In the graveyard, my people melt back into the ground, sighing sadly as they return to their earthbound sleep. There they will rest until I summon them again. I love them and I love both worlds that I live in. I am blessed to have this special power. Is it wrong for me to want more?

26

Finch
June 12

The Sunday that changed everything started in a deceptively quiet way. We indulged ourselves by sleeping in, and then decided to attend the 11:00 a.m. service at St. James, the local AME church. The church services were both a nice change of pace and a good way to strengthen our ties with the community. It was first Sunday, which meant the pastor, who worked on a circuit, would be at church, and attendance would be better than on other Sundays.

St. James was a small, sparkling white building from the nineteenth century, framed by large, heavy-limbed oaks. It was really just a large room filled with pews and lined with windows that were open wide to let in the breeze. As we entered, the choir was already singing, accompanied by someone playing a portable organ. Heads turned and I recognized some of the people I'd met since coming to St. Pierre. Not all expressions were welcoming, though, which reminded me that not everyone appreciated our persistent questions. Among the congregation members, I spotted Miss Myma, Sam Dent, and Caesar Cummings.

The choir sang a number of spirited old-time songs, and the congregation clapped and patted their feet in time.

Oh, the walk I used to walk,
I don't walk no more,
I don't walk no more,
I don't walk no more,
Oh, the walk I used to walk,
I don't walk no more,
Since the Lord laid his hand on me.
Oh, the talk I used to talk...

I settled in as the choir described several changes a person could go through: talking, singing, working...

Another song was slower, with a beautiful, haunting melody.

Come on in the room,
Come on in the room;
Jesus is my doctor;
He writes out my prescriptions,
In the room.

I could easily imagine the Black families of St. Pierre's earlier years finding solace and higher purpose in these simple but powerful messages of faith.

The pastor's sermon was on Jesus's miracles. He began by describing several of them, starting with the raising of the dead and the miracle of the loaves and fishes. Gradually, he became more and more animated, building toward a stirring crescendo:

"Go now, lawyers, and talk to this man Jesus!"
"Amen," the congregation said.
"We heard! We heard a man now heals the sick."
"He healed the sick!" they repeated.
"We heard he give sight to the blind!"
"The blind can see!"
"He open up the dumb ears."

"The deaf can hear!"

"He start the crippled to walkin'."

"The cripple can walk!"

"Same man!" the pastor shouted passionately, pounding on his lectern.

"Same man!" the congregation jubilantly shouted back.

"Same man!" the pastor repeated.

"Same man!" the voices responded.

"Same man!"

"Same man!"

The rhythm was hypnotic.

"He's comin' back one of these days."

"He's comin' back!"

"The same man this evenin'!"

"Jesus is comin' back!"

Mopping the perspiration from his forehead with a handkerchief,
the pastor fell silent, seemingly overcome with feeling. The organ-
ist maintained the rhythm of his words, interspersing the song with
snatches of others. Meanwhile, the congregation, on its feet, continued to shout, "Amen!"

It was an emotional climax that united everyone in extended jubi-
lation. Some "got the spirit" and were lowered back onto pews so that
they wouldn't fall on the ground. Others jumped up and down in
exaltation. This was my favorite part of the service, and I lost myself
in the moment. I was a fellow celebrant, not a researcher.

Gradually, the organ transitioned to a hymn that calmed the congregation's mood. Drying his face again, the pastor returned to the
pulpit and asked the ushers to pass the collection plates. Then he
asked visitors to introduce themselves. We all stood, and Elizabeth
spoke for the group.

"Good morning. My name is Elizabeth Wood. I'm a professor of
folklore at a university in Chicago. I've been visiting St. Pierre for
several years, and many of you have met me before." She smiled

broadly. Some people guardedly smiled back, while others watched her carefully.

"This year, I brought a team with me," Elizabeth continued. You've probably seen them walking on the road, and maybe you've talked to some of them too. This is Russell Bennett"—she gave him a little shove, and he smiled and nodded—"Sierra Jackman, and Finch Waters. We're interested in some of the old-time songs and stories that you learned from your parents and grandparents, and I hope you'll help us."

I saw a few people reaching for their necks, and noticed that some of them were wearing the strange amulets that protected Caesar and Myma.

After church, we had a big Sunday dinner and then relaxed on the front porch, waving at people who were walking up and down the road visiting their friends. I kept a sharp eye out for possible ghosts, but everyone and everything checked out fine. It was the last time that would ever be true, as things turned out.

27

Finch

June 12

That afternoon, the three of us read on the porch, enjoying a slight breeze that lifted the leaves from time to time. Elizabeth was down at Mrs. Taylor's store, using the phone.

A while later, she returned and asked, "Is anybody interested in finding the place where Big Jack was buried?"

"Are you serious?" Russell said. "Didn't you tell us that the slaves wouldn't go to that spot?"

"Yes, well that was a long time ago," she answered. "It's probably just an old superstition. I think that as long as we've made so much progress, we should try to find the spot where—what does the song say?—'The salt marsh meets the tide.'"

"There are a *lot* of salt marshes around here. How will we find the right one?" Sierra complained. Her legs were not as red and swollen as they'd been, but the ant bites were taking a long time to subside. That morning, she'd said that her legs still felt funny sometimes, like there was something crawling under her skin.

"That's probably just the heat," Elizabeth had suggested. "I wouldn't worry about it."

"They aren't *your* legs," Sierra had commented under her breath.

Now Sierra was rubbing her legs with rubbing alcohol and angling them to catch the cooling breeze.

"How will we find the right one?" Elizabeth repeated. "We're going to get some help from my friend Sam Dent."

Her friend. I glanced at Russell and Sierra to see if they reacted to the term, but their faces were blank. I remembered my dancing partner Andre at Sally's Club saying he'd seen Elizabeth and Sam walking around the marshes like they were looking for something.

Maybe an hour later, Caesar Cummings pulled into the driveway, accompanied by Sam Dent. They were both still wearing the suits they'd had on in church. Sam was also sporting the style of dark fedora that my grandfather would call a stingy brim.

Walking with his characteristically stiff and formal gait, Caesar paused at the bottom of the porch steps and said, "Good afternoon," with a little dip of his head.

"Good afternoon, Mr. Cummings," we said in chorus.

"I brought my friend Sam Dent," he said, looking around as though unsure whether or not we knew Sam.

Elizabeth stepped forward and said warmly, "Thanks, Caesar. The team met Sam at Sally's Club the other night." Sam extended his hand, looking at us intently; he was as alert as Caesar was distant.

"Elizabeth told me about your research on Big Jack and his song, and I think I might be able to help," Sam said, leaning comfortably on the porch railing.

"Don't you want to sit down?" Elizabeth asked him.

"No, I'm fine," he said, and Caesar nodded in agreement.

"We tell some pretty wild stories around here," Sam continued. "What have you found out about Big Jack?" He had a southern accent, but not the local one. His dark eyes met mine and I looked away uncomfortably. It felt like he was looking into my brain.

"We have four verses of the song so far," Elizabeth answered. I looked over at Sierra and Russell and smiled. We were all proud of the progress we'd made since the first week.

Elizabeth recited:

Big Jack had a secret book
He did; yes, he did
He kept it by his side
He did; yes, he did
He lived beside the water
He did; yes, he did
Where the salt marsh meets the tide
He did; yes, he did
Massa murdered Big Jack
He did; yes, he did
For wanting to be free
He did; yes, he did
He cut him into pieces,
Yes, he did; yes, he did
And threw him in the sea
Yes, he did; yes, he did.

"You're missing the tune," Sam said. This was news to me; no one else had ever mentioned that there was one. Ignoring the surprise on our faces, he marked the rhythm on his knee and sang the four verses back to us. The tune was melancholy and plaintive, like the words themselves. I could easily imagine the slaves who witnessed Big Jack's death singing this mournful melody as they sat in their cabins at night.

"That's a wonderful addition to our research!" Elizabeth ex-claimed. "I want to tape it."

Sam sang the tune twice for Elizabeth and then asked, "So what do you know about Big Jack's book?"

I thought I heard Elizabeth give a little gasp, but she said coolly, "Well, the story I heard about Big Jack was that he had a treasure, so I think 'book' is just a mistake that got into the song somehow." Sam pursed his thin lips and didn't respond.

Elizabeth turned to us and said, "According to the song, Big Jack was buried where the salt marsh meets the tide, but that could be anywhere along this coastline. Sam and I searched around a little bit last year, but we didn't have any luck finding anything. Now Sam says he thinks he knows where to look. "

"Actually, I have a pretty good idea about where we can find Big Jack's remains," Sam asserted confidently.

"I could take you and your students there if you want," he said. "But you have to be brave," he added, as he looked at each of us with his penetrating eyes.

Brave. I wondered what exactly he meant by that.

Russell spoke up immediately. "Count me in!" he announced. I figured he wanted to show off his manly courage. Sierra and I looked at each other uncertainly.

"Yes, we'll go with you," Elizabeth offered without asking us if we really wanted to do it. "We've come this far; why not see what we can find?"

"We have to go at night," Sam said. "In fact, tonight is good timing, because the full moon will make it easier to see. I'll come back to get you at nine. Wear clothes that can get muddy."

He turned to go, and Caesar Cummings turned with him. As I watched them walk to Caesar's car, I thought that Sam oddly reminded me of someone I'd read about or seen somewhere. And I remembered suddenly that Caesar hadn't stuttered when he was introducing us. Was that because he felt more at ease with Sam Dent than he did with us, or was it something else?

28

Finch

June 12

Punctually at nine, Sam Dent drove up to the house behind the wheel of a rather battered old truck. He was still wearing his stingy brim but had traded his Sunday suit for dark work clothes and rubber boots. It seemed like an odd combination to me, but no matter; it wasn't my concern. The full moon silvered the leaves overhead, and they rustled as though they were whispering secretly. For a moment I thought I saw a few of the ghostly green lights we'd seen the first night, off in the distance. The chattering and chirping of unseen insects, night birds, and frogs filled the hot air. My stomach tightened in anticipation of whatever we were about to do that required starting out at night and being brave.

There was only enough room for Elizabeth in the cab of Sam's truck, so the three of us rode together in the cargo section. Just before we climbed in, Sam reached into one of his pockets and removed some small objects.

"Here," he said, "put this on," and he turned to me with a stringed object in his hands. I smelled a familiar pungent odor, and my stomach churned: it was a garlic necklace like the one Caesar wore.

"Don't be afraid; this will protect you," Sam whispered in my ear as he tied the cord around my neck. Then he turned to Sierra, Russell, and Elizabeth and put garlic necklaces on them too.

"Look," he said, in his normal speaking voice, "each of you gets a different color. White for Elizabeth, yellow for Sierra, pink for Russell—"

"Pink?" Russell interjected. "Ew!"

"...and blue for Finch."

"Well, at least we'll know how to find each other in the dark," I joked weakly, as the truck bumped along the country roads and we scraped our knees against its sides and crashed into each other. It was not a pleasant ride.

Sam stopped when the road turned to sand and told us we'd have to walk the rest of the way.

"Where are we going?" Sierra asked.

"To where the salt marsh meets the tide," he said, laughing. "Because of the full moon, the tide will be out, and it will be easier for us to search the coastline." That sounded reasonable.

We trudged down the road; almost immediately sand got in my shoes, and I wished I'd worn my boots. Except for the invisible chattering night creatures, it seemed like we were completely alone. No lights signaled that there were houses nearby, no sounds indicated that people were staying cool on their porches, and no dogs rushed to ward us off.

Eventually, we passed the dark shape of a two-story building next to a huge, shadowy oak. "This is where I live," Sam said, looking my way.

"Here?" I asked. "It's so remote."

"I like it that way," he said with a small smile. As my eyes adjusted to the moonlight, I realized that white headstones surrounded his house. Pitted with age, they were arranged in irregular rows and had the appearance of uneven teeth emerging from the ground.

"Are we in a cemetery?" I asked with a panicky voice.

Sam gave a little laugh. "Ha! Yes, I like it here. It's peaceful, and people don't bother me."

"People say that spirits walk in the graveyard during the full moon," Elizabeth said a little nervously, as we began to walk through the gravestones.

"Well, that might be so," Sam said vaguely.

"Are you saying that's true, that there are spirits out there?" Sierra asked. Her voice quavered, and I knew she was afraid. I was getting spooked too.

Sam said, "The spirits won't hurt you if you know what to do, so you have to follow my directions." This was not reassuring. He was acting like the spirits were real. Were they, or was he just trying to scare us?

"Hey, man," Russell said, "are you serious?"

"Yes," Sam said firmly. "Now follow me, and do exactly what I tell you to do."

I looked back over at Elizabeth. Now she didn't seem afraid; in fact, she seemed *excited*. Her eyes were shining, and she was almost smiling. "Come on, kids," she said. "We need to stick together."

Sam took the lead walking through the gravestones, signaling with a finger against his lips that we should be quiet. The ground was soft and uneven, and we walked slowly. What if I fell into an old grave? Something touched my face, and I jumped involuntarily and tried to stifle a scream. It turned out to be just moss, but at first it had felt like fingers softly caressing my cheek. Sam turned at the stifled sound, his finger raised to his lips again.

We trudged on through the gravestones, along the seemingly endless path. Once, I thought I heard a distant voice calling, "Finch," and I looked around quickly in the silvery darkness, my heart beating faster. The voice—or whatever it was—had come from a pool of darkness under some trees, and no one else seemed to have heard it. We walked on in silence, single file, heading for an unknown destination.

Now I heard the voice again. This time it was louder. Soon other voices joined it. The strange chorus got louder, and gradually the voices combined in a blood-chilling sound that rose through the trees like an unearthly, wordless scream.

We stopped and looked fearfully toward the impenetrable, shadowy trees that surrounded us. Suddenly, misty vapors engulfed us, as the wild scream continued in the background. The vapors swirled around our heads and then gradually transformed into faces, the tortured, leathery brown faces of adults, old people, and children.

Were we walking in a slave graveyard? A chill ran up my spine as the faces twisted around me, and my scalp crawled. Frozen in my steps, first I saw the shrieking head of someone whose eyes had been gouged out; then another face with mangled flesh where there used to be ears. A third face was obscured with blood. I cringed as the faces rose and fell around us, shrieking in their endless sorrow. Then, I heard another cry, closer than the dreadful sound that already filled my ears. It was Sierra, who was screaming in terror.

"No sound!" Sam shouted, as though he was unconcerned about Sierra. "We have to hurry now, before…"

He started running, and I tried to follow, but strangely I couldn't move. I looked down: a root as thick as my wrist had emerged from the earth and was beginning to twine itself around my foot. I tugged as hard as I could and still couldn't move. I pulled even harder and saw, to my horror, a ghostly gray hand emerge from the hole where the root had been. My heart pounded. What was the use of the garlic? We were going to die!

The hand grabbed my foot and began to pull me toward the ground. I fought to stay upright and fell sideways. More roots and hands grabbed at my hands and my face. I screamed and writhed, fighting for my life. My head rang with the unearthly sound of the ghostly screams, as dirt filled my mouth and threatened to choke me.

I don't know how long I struggled like that. To me, it felt like an eternity, but it could have been just minutes. Then I sensed that Sam was nearby. Still struggling, I saw that he had a large knife like a machete in his hand. With strong strokes, Sam used the machete to slash me free from the grasping roots. With the same blade, he hacked at the misty hands, and in reaction moans and shrieks came up from the earth.

Sam pulled me up roughly onto my feet and gave me a shove.

"Run straight ahead to the water," he shouted in my ear, pointing ahead of me.

The wild shrieking was still coming from under the trees, and the hideous, tormented faces swam in front of me. I pushed myself past them, lost my footing on one of the gravestones, and fell.

Terrified that more roots and hands would capture me, I desperately scrambled up and ran in the direction Sam had pointed. As I did so, I saw him leaning over Sierra, frantically cutting her free from some of the roots with slicing blows of his knife. She was crying hysterically. Her body was almost covered by a seething mass of brown roots and gray hands. As my brain swirled, I wondered briefly why the roots and hands didn't attack Sam, but in the moment there wasn't time to think about it.

29

Finch
June 12

Running for my life from the terrors of the graveyard, I smelled the salt creek before I saw it. Somehow, that familiar damp rankness was comforting after everything I'd been through. Slowing my pace so that I wouldn't fall in the water by mistake, I found Russell and Elizabeth standing by the creek's edge. Silhouetted by the moonlight, they were bent over in exhaustion and panting for breath. For a while, we were all too winded to speak. Finally, Sam came along, leading Sierra by the hand. She too was trying to catch her breath. Her hair was wild, and her face was contorted and wet with tears.

"What happened?" I gasped. "What were those voices and those faces?"

Sam shook his head. "Those are slave spirits that were never buried properly," he said. "When those slaves died, their bodies were just dumped into the creek. They rise from the shadows when they are disturbed. You see how they look. Like Big Jack they died horrendous deaths."

"What about the vines and those horrible hands?" Russell demanded angrily. "What was that about? We could have been killed!"

Calmly—too calmly?—Sam explained, "The graveyard rises up to protect the spirits that live there. That's why I wanted you to be quiet."

"Why didn't those things come after you?" Russell asked, persisting.

"They know me because I live among them," Sam answered.

As I regained my composure, anger began to replace fear. "Why didn't those necklaces protect us?" I asked Sam. "Isn't that what the garlic is for?"

"No, the garlic is for protection from what comes next," he replied grimly. "Come on, we have to keep moving." I felt my composure fading again.

Sam led us to three small canoe-like boats that were tied up at an old rickety dock by the side of the creek. We had seen local fisherman in this style of boat before. Sam climbed into one of them and pushed off into the muddy water. Quickly, Sierra and I got into one of the remaining boats, and Russell and Elizabeth got into the third one.

Paddling behind Sam, we followed the current made by the retreating tide as it led toward the open water of the ocean. A wavy path of moonlight shimmered before us, occasionally broken by the creepy, curving shapes of snakes. There were disturbing shadows under the trees by the side of the creek, and from time to time I heard splashing sounds that made me wonder if something was following us in the water. I was terrified.

I couldn't see Sierra's face because I was sitting behind her, but her back and neck were visibly stiff and tense, and she was still sniffing.

"Sierra," I said softly, "are you okay?" She turned and looked at me over her shoulder, her face tight with fear.

"I want to get out of here," she said. "I want to go home; don't you?"

"Yeah," I agreed, "me too." If I could have called my parents or a friend right then, I would have. But of course I couldn't. I felt trapped and alone.

Eventually, Sam stopped paddling. In the moonlit darkness I saw him signal for us to come closer. Our boats bumped together as we clustered near his, making hollow knocking sounds like a waterlogged heartbeat. Behind us were the long grasses of the salt marshes and

the moonlit path through them that we had followed. Before us, I saw
the open waters of the ocean. To our right there was a little island,
separated by the water from others that were closer to the shore.

"This is the island where Big Jack and some other slaves lived,"
Sam said. "We'll walk the rest of the way to his cabin. The water's not
too deep in low tide. It's muddy though. Take off your shoes and roll
up your pants."

"There are snakes in this water," Russell protested. "Can your garlic protect us from them?" Sam ignored him and slid from his boat
into the water, bringing a bulky tool bag with him.

The boat rocked as Sierra and I clambered out, and I hoped it
wouldn't overturn; falling into the creek was the last thing I needed.
I took off my shoes, rolled my pants up, and stepped into lukewarm
water that came up to my knees. The marshy mud squished uncomfortably between my toes, and with a shiver I felt something swim
past my feet. We tied our boat to a rotting piece of wood that must
have been part of a dock at one time and followed Sam in single file
toward the island.

Soon we entered a little clearing under the trees where, to my surprise, an old cabin still stood. It consisted of one or two small rooms
with a damaged, deeply slanting roof and a single chimney. The walls
were made of oyster shells and clay and glowed with an eerie white
light in the moonlight.

Sam stopped in front of the cabin, and we clustered around him.
"I think Big Jack hid his book in this house," he said simply.

"Do you think it could still be here?" Elizabeth asked. Her eyes
had that excited look again. She was so focused on the chase that she
hadn't asked any of us how we were doing, which I didn't like. And
why hadn't she corrected Sam the way she had before, when she said
that Big Jack had hidden Massa's treasure, not a book? Did it make a
difference?

"What makes you think the book, or treasure, or whatever it is
we're looking for is here?" Sierra asked Sam with a voice that only
slightly betrayed how frightened I knew she was.

"Ever since I first heard the song about Big Jack, I've wondered where he lived," Sam answered. "So I did some historical research on my own. And Elizabeth and I poked around last summer when she was here." He looked briefly in her direction and smiled. "I'm pretty sure we're in the right place tonight."

As Sam walked down the short shell path to the house, I thought I heard him mumble something like, "But I didn't have everything I needed before; now I have what I need," and I wondered what he meant. He pushed open the cabin door, which leaned sideways on ancient hinges. I clutched the garlic necklace at my throat and wondered what awaited us inside.

30

Finch

June 12

Inside Big Jack's cabin, there was thick darkness. A little moonlight fil-
tered in through the broken roof and the window openings, enough
to see the outline of the room and some piles of clothes or bedding
on the floor. It smelled terrible. The odor was more than mustiness,
and more like something was rotting all around us. Had some kind
of wild animal dragged a carcass into the cabin?

"If Big Jack lived back in the seventeen hundreds, how could his
cabin still be here?" Russell asked as we peered around. Sam didn't
answer.

"Sam!" Russell said with a sharper tone. "Why is this cabin still
here?"

"Because no one used it after Big Jack died. The slaves said the
island was cursed," Sam answered almost casually, glancing over his
shoulder at Russell.

"What?" Russell muttered.

My heart gave a frightened thud. Disturbingly, I thought I saw
shadowy forms stirring in the gloomy corners of the room. Animals?
Something else?

"Make sure your necklaces have a tight knot and follow me," Sam
said sharply. "Don't ask any more questions; just do what I say."

From one of his pockets, he produced a small flashlight that provided just enough light to show us where to walk. The corners of the room were still in shadows.

We followed Sam through the front room into a second area that seemed even darker, if that was possible, and made me feel like I was in a tomb. Here, there were no windows to let in the outside light. The darkness was almost palpable, and the stench was so strong that I could barely breathe.

"Jeez," Russell said softly. "This is unbearable."

"Shh!" Sam responded sharply, as he led us deeper toward the corner of the room.

As we crept forward, I thought I heard something, and my heart sank in dread of another experience like the one in the graveyard. The sound came from above us...no, below us...no, all around us. It grew gradually louder like the footsteps of an advancing army. Soon, the very air reverberated with a strange moaning that crescendoed until it canceled out all the other night sounds.

The moaning swirled around our heads and beat at our ears. It began as a lonely, sad sound and then gradually began to sound familiar. Bizarrely, I suddenly recognized one of the hymns we'd heard Sunday morning in church.

"Come on in the room," the voices intoned, and then again.

Come on in the room.

Over and over, unseen presences repeated the phrase.

Come on in the room.

Come on in the room.

Was I going crazy? I looked in panic at the others, whose faces were dimly visible in the light reflected by the shells from the flashlight's beam. The fear I saw in their eyes told me they could hear the song too...was that a good sign? Who or what was in the cabin with us?

Church...Sunday morning...all that felt like a year ago. I stole a glance at the glowing dial of my watch; it was just past midnight now.

Clapping and stamping now joined with the eerie voices, just as it had accompanied the singing in church. The floor and walls shook with the sound. I looked into Sierra's frightened face; she was covering her ears. Russell and Elizabeth were holding hands and probably didn't even know it. I put my arm around Sierra and wished someone could make *me* feel safe.

The song grew even louder, but Sam seemed unfazed.

"Sam, what are those voices?" Elizabeth shouted over the cacophony. He ignored her and crouched down in a corner of the cabin, where he began to dig with a small pointed trowel that must have been in his bag.

"Come on, help me," he shouted over his shoulder. "Use your hands!"

Dutifully, I crouched down in the stinking air and helped Sam widen the hole he was digging. I felt like a dog searching for a bone as crusty dirt pushed under my fingernails. Almost immediately, my palms were cut by pieces of oyster shell, and soon the cuts began to sting. Meanwhile, the wild singing, clapping, and foot stomping continued, as though a ghostly army were coming to get us. The hymn had sounded friendly and comforting in church on Sunday, but now it was deafening and horrible. *Come on in the room*—were we being lured to our deaths?

Through the din, we all heard a sharp sound as Sam's trowel struck something metallic. He signaled sharply for us to stop digging.

"What was that?" Elizabeth asked.

Sam didn't answer and continued digging on his own, carefully opening a space around whatever he'd found. Finally, he reached into the hole and extracted a metal box that had turned green with tarnish and age. The box was unmarked and nondescript. Could it be the treasure we'd heard about?

Still crouched in the corner, with the four of us gathered around him, Sam used his trowel to force the box open. Flakes of green fell off, and the metal screeched. Inside, there was a small bundle wrapped in an ancient woven cloth. The cloth was still intact, but it had been eaten away in places by bugs or rot.

Sam began carefully unwrapping the bundle, which was about the size of a bag of coins or a book. The voices surrounding us were unimaginably loud. With part of my brain, I registered that now I was hearing a new, wordless song that sounded vaguely African.

Suddenly, a blood-curdling scream soared above the new sound. The scream was far from otherworldly; it was human and close by.

Turning, I saw that Sierra had fallen to the ground. I moved toward her to help her to her feet and was shocked to see that her skin was writhing, as though she was having massive muscle spasms. As she twisted and screamed, the skin of her arms and legs rippled just as if something was moving beneath it. I knelt beside her, looking on helplessly and wondering what to do. The ripples grew larger and moved more forcefully. It appeared that an imprisoned force was trying to escape from inside her body.

To my horror, a scaly green head suddenly protruded from the skin of her arm and turned its red eyes toward me. I quickly recoiled and fell backward. Then, as Sierra screamed and screamed, her terrified voice rising above the relentless voices of the unseen presences, snakes began emerging from every part of her body. Evil snake heads poked from her arms and legs, from her mouth and nose, and even from her eye sockets. Their tongues flickered and their eyes gleamed red in the dark. Long, scaly bodies followed the malevolent heads and coiled vertically in the air above her body, which now lay silently still. Others slithered on the ground next to her, their tails still embedded disgustingly in her flesh.

I wanted to run far from that nightmare place, but I had to save Sierra. Kneeling again, I began to reach for her, but Sam stopped me with his arm.

"We have to get out of here," he said harshly. "There's nothing we can do to help her."

I didn't understand. What about the garlic? Why hadn't it protected Sierra? Her face was gone now, swallowed up in a mass of slithering snakes' heads. It was a horrible sight, but I reached toward her again, thinking that I could kill the snakes.

"No!" Sam said sharply, shoving me backward. "We have to go."

I looked desperately for Russell, but he was no use. In the dim light I saw him standing a few feet from Sierra's body, seemingly frozen, staring aghast at the mass of thrashing snakes.

Strangely enough, Elizabeth wasn't even looking at Sierra, much less trying to rescue her. Instead, she stared hungrily at the bundle in Sam's hands.

"We have to go!" Sam repeated. He jerked Elizabeth's hand and began walking quickly toward the front of the cabin.

At that moment, the ground began heaving beneath our feet. At first, it was a subtle rocking motion, like an earthquake. I struggled to keep my footing and saw that all of us were swaying unsteadily. Then the walls shook violently, and pieces of oyster shell rained on our heads. Fearfully, I looked around me, my heart pounding. The cabin was crumbling around us!

Amid the chaos of the collapsing cabin and the ongoing dissonance of voices, clapping, and stomping, I saw Sam drop the bundle. Some of the cloth came loose, and I could clearly see part of an old leather-bound book. So the song was right: Big Jack had hidden a book, not a stolen treasure.

I shouted at Elizabeth, "Can't we save Sierra?"

She shook her head, and I saw her reach toward the book. Now? This wasn't the time for that! Sam saw her too, and he quickly scooped it up and put it in his shirt. Then he grabbed her hand again, and we ran together from the cabin.

Behind us, it crumbled to the ground with a noisy crash that released a cloud of silvery pulverized shells. Then there was an eerie silence. No African voices, no clapping, no stomping—not even the night noises of insects and frogs disturbed the aftermath of the cabin's destruction. There were just the occasional sounds the rubble released as it settled into the earth.

I don't remember much about how we got back to St. Pierre. I recall paddling with the tide, which was coming back in now. The snakes in the water didn't frighten me anymore. I didn't care about the shadows under the trees. I was in shock from what had happened to us and to Sierra. My head pounded so hard I could barely think, and my throat hurt from shouting. I felt empty and defeated. I guess we all did, because no one spoke.

Silently, we crossed the salt creek and landed at the dock. The moon was setting now. Vaguely, because it felt like my brain wasn't working anymore, I heard the chirping of the first birds greeting the rising sun. We trudged down the path through the graveyard. Now that it was dawn, there were no signs of the roots and ghostly hands. There were no shadowy shapes, and it was silent. It was almost as though the events of the night hadn't happened—except that we were returning without Sierra. Silently, Elizabeth, Russell, and I got into Sam's truck, and he dropped us off at the house.

31

Elizabeth
June 12

Sam called after church to finalize the arrangements for our trip to find Big Jack's cabin. It was time, he said, because the moon was full.

At first, everything went according to plan. During the afternoon, he stopped by with Caesar and "volunteered" to take us to find Big Jack's cabin. He knew Big Jack's song as well as I did, but he played along with me by singing only part of it to the kids and not correcting me when I said we were looking for treasure, not a book.

When he said he'd be back for us at nine, I wondered again why we were going at night. I didn't buy his story that he wanted privacy. That could be part of it, but I sensed there was more to his reason than that. It bothered me that I didn't know what was going on—and that he refused to share his information with me. Weren't we supposed to be in this together?

That night, riding with Sam in the cab of his truck, I didn't ask many questions because the kids might have been able to hear us. I didn't want them to find out that Sam and I knew more of the Big Jack story than we'd been letting on. I stared out of the open window as the truck bumped along, wondering what lay ahead of us. Could this really be the night that would answer my questions about the book of secrets? Sam reached over and squeezed my hand a few times, but otherwise he was quiet too.

I was surprised when the truck stopped near his creepy house in the graveyard. I'd been there before, on previous visits to the island, but never at night.

"What are we doing here?" I asked, looking over at him.

"Well, as it turns out, Big Jack's cabin was closer than we thought. All we have to do is cross the graveyard, and then we can take canoes from there." *All we have to do is cross the graveyard*...the thought gave me chills.

"We're crossing a graveyard at night?" I asked, trying unsuccessfully to conceal my fear.

"Don't worry, babe," he said. "You'll be okay if you stick with me." As it turned out, that assurance worked for Russell, Finch, and me, but hardly for Sierra.

Looking back on everything that happened that night at Big Jack's cabin, I understand now that finding the book of secrets required...let's call it an exchange. You could use the word "sacrifice" too. Maybe it was only fair. After all, everything has a price. How could we get something as monumental as the book of secrets without giving something back in return?

Sorry, Sierra. It's too bad that you ended up paying the price for our ambition, but that was Sam's doing, not mine, right? I trusted him—"Bring a team," he said—and then by the time I understood what was going on, it was too late to do anything about it. Events had taken their course. At any rate, that's how it seemed to me when I thought about it later. And if I was completely honest with myself, even if I felt bad about you, I was also excited by the prospects of having—and owning—the book of secrets...once I got it from Sam.

But I've gotten ahead of myself. The strange night that was such a deadly turning point began in earnest when Sam parked the truck near his house and handed out the protective amulets. At the time, I wasn't sure if I believed the one he handed me had any power. This was the thing about St. Pierre: you were surrounded by people who believed in otherworldly spirits and ghosts—who would point at someone walking down the road and tell you it wasn't a person; it was a ghost—and you had to decide if there was any truth in what they were saying or if it was just superstition. I know better now, but on that night I was still uncertain. Anyway, to play it safe, I went along with Sam and tied the amulet around my neck.

When Sam first took me to his house a few years ago, I was dismayed to find out he lived in a graveyard. "You live *here*?" I asked him in surprise. He answered, "I like it here. It's quiet, and people don't bother me." What seemed quiet to him was disturbing to me, but those previous visits were in the daytime, so I didn't have to think about it too much. Now, threading our way under the moonlight, I didn't feel so good about walking through all those graves. It was spooky, and there were things going on that bothered me, like the movements in the shadows that I saw out of the corner of my eye.

"People tell me that spirits walk in the graveyard during the full moon," I said to Sam as we started out along a dimly visible path.

"Well...that might be so," he replied vaguely. It was one of his typical, infuriatingly ambiguous responses. I tried not to show my feelings, for the sake of the kids. And I tried to look calm, because I saw they were getting nervous. Sam saw that too and assured them that the spirits wouldn't hurt them if they followed his directions.

When I joined in by encouraging the team to stick together, I saw Finch looking at me suspiciously, as though I'd betrayed her. I guess she was surprised that I wasn't as terrified as she was. But, truth be told, I was excited about our adventure. Sure, the darkness and strange rustlings under the trees were frightening, but I was thrilled by the thought that my years of searching might finally be over. I had no idea what the book of secrets contained—or if it even existed—but for me the opportunity to find out was absolutely intoxicating.

It's too bad my exhilaration didn't last. Our trip through the graveyard was so horrifying that I was afraid for my life. And it dismissed any doubts I had about the reality of spirits and ghosts.

To get to the water's edge, we followed Sam down an uneven path that wound through the irregularly scattered gravestones. Even though the full moon was bright and Sam had a flashlight, the grave-yard was still so shadowy that I could barely see to walk. I had to look down to keep from tripping, which made it hard to follow Sam.

We were slowly stumbling along in single file when there was a strange sound from somewhere in the shadows. At first I thought it was the wind. Then the sound got louder, and I realized it was voices, bone-chilling voices. Was it possibly a natural phenomenon like birds or wild animals? No, these were human voices, echoing with wild fury and deep sorrow and rising into a terrifying chorus of screams.

Instinctively, we began walking faster—or tried to—but soon we encountered strange misty vapors. They gradually merged into faces that were so twisted and mangled that I *knew* they belonged to people who had died in slavery. These were the faces of people who had lived and died in pain. They rose and fell around me as though floating in the wind, their black eyes staring into mine. They came closer and closer, and I struck out wildly to push them away. But my hands passed through them, and they swirled away into the air like fog. Then they materialized again and swirled and swarmed toward my face.

I flailed at them over and over with both arms, still stumbling for-ward on the path. All around us were the shrieking voices, and then I thought I heard one of the kids' voices too. I suddenly felt encircle my waist and I screamed in fright. It was Sam. He held my arms down by my side and whispered hoarsely, "Stop fighting them, Elizabeth. They are not your enemies. They're trying to tell you their stories. Just run to the water and don't look back. I've given you special protection."

I ran blindly, tripping repeatedly on the uneven ground and fall-ing over protruding gravestones. On one fall, I hit my head on a stone and lay on the ground, disoriented, trying to get my bearings. As I did, I felt something rough and rope-like wrapping itself around my wrist. Screaming in absolute terror, I pulled sharply upward and managed to free myself. Meanwhile, behind me, I heard a shrieking, panicked yell, and thought I recognized Sierra's voice. *Don't look back,* I told myself. I hoped that Sam would help her.

I kept running, out of breath but afraid to stop. I felt like I was in a nightmare, running as hard as I could but not getting anywhere. I heard steps behind me and ragged breathing. "Sam?" I called out over my shoulder.

"No, it's me, Russell." There was desperation in his voice. "I need your help."

I stopped and Russell ran toward me, his shirt torn and blood on his face. His hands were pulling frantically at a thick vine that was wrapped several times around his neck, with one end writhing in the air like a snake.

"Help me!" he cried in a choked voice. I ran to his side, and together we pulled frantically at the twisting vine. It was rough and warm like a horrible, alien arm.

It took what seemed like an eternity, but eventually I was able to bend the vine and snap it in two. It screamed when I did that with what sounded like a human voice. One part slithered down Russell's body and crawled along the ground like a snake. Just before it disappeared into the ground, I had the dreadful impression that I'd seen *fingers.*

Russell was choking and gasping for breath, but I knew that we needed to keep moving. I grabbed his hand, and together we ran toward the water's edge.

There was no one there. For a panicked moment, I was afraid that only Russell and I had survived the terrible trip across the graveyard. My heart pounded, and I gasped for breath, desperately hoping that I was wrong.

Meanwhile, in another part of my mind, it sank in that the supernatural stories people had been telling me weren't just folktales. Unless I'd gone crazy in the last hour, another world existed that I'd never accepted as real before. But clearly it was. And what, I wondered, was Sam's relationship to this other world? Was he one of the occult practitioners that local people called root doctors? If so, he'd never said anything about that to me. Yet he seemed to have some kind of mysterious powers.

The sound of approaching footsteps jerked me out of my thoughts and back into the present. Russell and I tensed and exchanged frightened looks, which turned to relief as first Finch emerged from the engulfing darkness and then Sam, who was leading Sierra by the hand.

We were all dirty and disheveled. Our clothes were torn and our expressions were wild. Sierra was crying. Only Sam was relatively untouched...which led my thoughts to the same question that Russell asked him: "Why didn't those things come after you?"

Sam's answer—"They know me because I live among them"—confirmed my theory that there was something he wasn't telling me. I didn't say anything right then, but I vowed I would find out more.

Paddling across the creek with Russell, I felt calmer, and my excitement about our journey returned. I was amazed that Sam had found Big Jack's cabin. Even knowing the name and site of the plantation where he'd lived, there were still acres and acres of uninhabited land where the cabin could have been located. Something told me that Sam had lied to me about how he'd discovered the cabin, but I brushed away the thought. If he was right, did I care about his methods?

As we pushed through dark underbrush that I would guess hadn't been disturbed in decades, if not centuries, I felt my heart beating faster with anticipation. The hunt was on! Eventually we arrived at a little clearing and the remains of a small cabin. It was made of broken oyster shells and resembled surviving slave cabins that I'd seen on other parts of St. Pierre. We stopped and stared at it, each one of us no doubt wondering what we would find within. Sam pointed at the cabin and said, "I think Big Jack left his book in this house."

I was so excited that I forgot to "correct" him by saying it was treasure, not a book. Instead, I slipped up and asked, "Do you think it could still be here?" I looked around quickly after that, wondering if anyone had noticed my blunder, but it was too dark to read their expressions.

It was as terrifying inside the cabin as it had been in the graveyard—and mentally I cursed Sam for not warning me about what he was going to put us through. To begin with, it stank inside the cabin, horribly. What could smell that foul? It couldn't possibly be organic. I didn't react—*must stay strong for the team*—but I feared the odor was part of Sam's supernatural world, and that soon we would encounter more of that mysterious world.

Sure enough, next came the demonically twisted song that surrounded us on all sides. *Come on in the room,* the spectral voices repeated, growing louder and louder, until I thought I would lose my mind. For an awful moment, I imagined that I would never leave that reeking, abysmally dark room with the shifting shadows in the corners. This was it: this was where my quest for the book of secrets would end. My shoulder brushed someone else's, and I instinctively grasped the nearby hand. It was Russell's, and just like in the graveyard, our touch was a brief comfort in this alien, otherworldly hell.

Sam seemed unfazed by the noise and smells. *This is his world,* I thought with a chill. Over the cacophony, I shouted, "Sam, what are those voices?" but he ignored me. Instead, he crouched down in one corner of the room and began digging with a sharp tool he'd brought with him.

"Come on, help me," he ordered us. "Use your hands!"

The five of us dug furiously, seemingly oblivious to the crazy voices that never stopped singing—if that's what you could call it—and the noxious smells; it must have been a bizarre scene. And oddly enough, I was proud of my team, even though I had completely misled them about the purpose of our mission. They were doing what I had asked them to do, and I appreciated that.

And so we widened the hole that Sam had started, until I distinctly heard his tool strike something metallic. He abruptly signaled for us to stop, and I asked, "What was that?"

Okay, it was a rhetorical question. But he could have answered. Instead, he ignored me just like before—*shithead*—and continued digging carefully and slowly, as he zeroed in on his target.

By the time Sam pulled the tarnished box from the hole, my heart was pounding so hard that my chest reverberated with the dull thuds. The box was unmarked and nondescript, but even before Sam opened it I was certain we'd find a book—*the book*—inside.

Anticipation ran through me like a shot of adrenaline, and I had to force myself to calm down. I took several deep breaths, mentally bracing myself each time for the horrible smell that made me want to gag. Meanwhile, Sam pried the metal box open and extracted a small bundle wrapped in an ancient woven cloth. The story about Big Jack said that he had wrapped his book in a woven cloth. We'd found the book of secrets, I was sure of it!

That's when everything went crazy with Sierra. At first I just stared, like everyone else, and watched in horror as her body was transformed into a writhing mass of snakes. The St. Pierre people believed that a root doctor could make you feel like there were snakes underneath your skin. Was that what was happening? But this clearly wasn't something psychological; these snakes were all too real. Could they be related to the feelings Sierra had in her legs after the ant attack? I couldn't sort it out—not now, at least, not with the book of secrets literally just inches away.

Sam probably could have helped Sierra, but he didn't even try to. I was watching him, and he never made a move in her direction. That's when I had my first inkling that for him, this was all going according to plan. He'd made some kind of deal—with the graveyard spirits? With somebody or something?—that was playing out in front of us. It was disgusting to think about, so I didn't. I focused instead on the book of secrets and my gratitude that Sam had figured out what we needed to do to get it.

Sam was holding the book. *When would he give it to me?*

Finch, my strongest team member, tried to help Sierra, but Sam stopped her. "We have to get out of here," he told her. "There's nothing we can do to help her."

I saw the pain and confusion on Finch's face, especially when Sam harshly repeated that we had to go. He jerked me toward the door—and just then the ground and walls began heaving around us. The dirt floor of the cabin rippled like water, and the walls creaked and released handfuls of oyster-shell fragments into the air. All too soon, it was clear that Big Jack's cabin was collapsing around us.

The movement of the cabin floor made it as hard to walk as on the rolling deck of a ship, and the sounds and smells made it equally hard to concentrate. In all the excitement, Sam dropped the bundle he'd taken from the box. When it hit the ground, the cloth shifted, and I could clearly see the cover of a leather-bound book.

I reached for it so it wouldn't get trampled or lost, but Sam snatched it up and put it in his shirt. Later, I replayed that moment over and over again in my mind. I didn't like the way he'd taken the book, not like he was keeping it safe, but more like he was keeping it out of my hands. *When will he give it to me?*

At the moment, I didn't have time to think. We had to escape the disintegrating cabin. Sam grabbed my hand again and we ran as fast as we could, trailed by the crash of the crumbling walls and splintering roof.

And then it was silent. After the cabin's total assault on our senses, the quiet was overwhelming. The noisy finale of our search had silenced even the night birds and animals. In silence, we rowed across the salt creek and picked our way through the graveyard. It was eerily calm in the first light of early dawn, and the ground was not even disturbed, as though the events of the night before had never happened.

On the drive back to the house, I realized for the first time how tired I was. In my exhausted mind, one phrase played over and over again: *When do I get the book?*

32

Finch

June 13

I remember falling across my bed—still in the clothes I'd worn to Big Jack's cabin—and sleeping until late into the morning. I was groggy and disoriented when I finally got up, until the stinking room slapped me back into reality. It reeked of mud, salt water, and fear-spawned sweat, all of which permeated my still-damp clothes. On top of that, my head hurt and my hands were cut, swollen, and throbbing. I was miserable and drained.

The memory of Sierra's death was like a pain in my chest that made it hard to breathe. I just wanted us to leave this godforsaken place and go home. No song was worth what we'd been through. No treasure—or book—was worth Sierra's death.

I desperately wanted to talk to my parents. I picked up my phone, knowing full well it wouldn't work, and threw it in frustration on the bed. The dead screen blindly rebuked me—with no signal, I hadn't even kept it charged. The thought of calling from the ratty phone at Taylor's store—with no privacy to boot—infuriated me.

Without thinking about Russell and Elizabeth, I stumbled out the back door to the pump. I splashed some ice-cold water into a basin that I took back to my room, hoping the cold shock would make me feel better. I peeled off my smelly clothes, which were stiffening from the mud and drying creek water, and washed myself thoroughly.

Afterward, I felt physically refreshed, although I was still deeply depressed and confused. What had happened to us in the graveyard and Big Jack's cabin? Were those shapes, sounds, and smells real? Were the ghosts and spirits we'd been hearing about from the local people *real*, or was there a rational explanation for what we'd experienced? One thing I knew for sure: Sierra's death was very real. The very thought of it was like a dense, heavy mass that clouded my mind.

I found Russell and Elizabeth sitting listlessly on the front porch, and without speaking I threw myself into one of the chairs and joined them.

"Can we leave now?" I asked Elizabeth after a while. "I hate it here; I want to go home."

"We have to find Sierra's body," she said dully. "Then there will be an inquiry. I guess the sheriff will conduct it, or the magistrate."

"Oh, great," I said bitterly. "Are we going to tell them that Sierra died because snakes came out of her? Or will we just say that we were looking for a treasure we heard about in a song?"

Elizabeth looked worried. "We're going to have to come up with some kind of story."

"*Some kind* of story?" I asked incredulously. "Why can't we tell them the truth?"

"Well…" she said and trailed off as though she was already working on what she was going to say.

"What about Sierra's parents? Don't you think we should tell them something?"

"I don't think we want to do that yet," Elizabeth said carefully. "Not if I'm just reporting her as missing. We don't want to cause any unnecessary, um, excitement."

"Yes, I guess there would be some *excitement* if Sierra's parents found out their daughter was dead," I said. "This situation is fucking unbelievable. And I'm not sure you care about her at all."

Elizabeth didn't answer. I looked over at Russell and saw that he was staring into space as though in shock.

I wanted to talk to my parents, but I also felt very tired. Too tired to move. I sat at the table with Elizabeth and Russell, listening to the hypnotic drone of the cicadas in the trees. The sound had a strangely calming effect.

Finally, I sighed and said, "I'm going to call home."

"Good idea. I will too," Russell said.

We walked down the road to Mrs. Taylor's store. I didn't feel like talking, and Russell was quiet too. We turned down the driveway to the store, and I saw, with a sinking heart, that the door was closed and the lights were off. I shook the knob a few times just to be sure, but it was locked tight. Russell and I looked at each other, feeling defeated. The Taylor's pay phone was the only one we knew about.

A car slowed near us, and a man I recognized from church shouted out the window, "Mrs. Taylor's at a funeral. The store will be open tomorrow."

So much for that. We started back down the road in the direction of the house.

"Russell, what are we going to do? Everything's gone crazy."

"I don't know. Do you think we should go home?"

"And just leave Sierra here?" It was really "Sierra's body," not "Sierra," but I wasn't ready for that. Better to talk about her as though she'd just dropped out of sight and might turn up again.

"If we left, do you think we could get blamed for…for what happened to her? Do you think someone would think we murdered her?"

Accused of murder. I hadn't thought of that. Down here, where we were strangers, that seemed very possible. "We're the only ones who know she's dead. I think we have to stay here for now. That's what Elizabeth said. She's going to file some kind of report with the magistrate, and we're going keep doing our research."

Later that afternoon, Elizabeth left to file the missing-person report with the magistrate. She seemed to think doing this would avoid the kinds of questions that would come up if she reported that Sierra had died.

While she was gone, Russell and I sat slumped on the porch. We barely had the energy to breathe, much less to do anything productive. I wondered if I should call Sierra's parents the next time Mrs. Taylor's store was open. Poor souls…they thought she would be coming home in a few weeks.

"Do you think that stuff we saw in the graveyard and on the island was real?" I asked Russell.

"I don't know. I don't know what to think. I mean—"

"I grew up believing ghosts and spirits were just old-time superstitions," I cut in, "but it sure seemed real to me."

"*Something* killed Sierra. Did you see those snakes?" He shivered. "It was like a nightmare, except it was real. We actually saw it happen."

"Do you think Sam could be fooling us somehow?"

"Like a magical trick of some kind?"

"It's just an idea," I said defensively. I wasn't ready to admit to myself that the world could be very, very different from what I'd been raised to believe it was.

"I sure wish we could leave," he said wistfully. "But I guess we have to stay for now."

He sighed and closed his eyes, looking tired and subtly older than he had just the day before.

I went into Sierra's room and packed her belongings and papers in her suitcases. She'd been full of excited anticipation on the drive south to St. Pierre, but once we got to the island, she'd had the toughest time of all of us. It had started with the ant bites, then the swollen legs, and now…this. A whiff of perfume from her clothes brought back a flood of vivid memories. Sierra slapping the fire ants…laughingly reporting on a research adventure…looking pretty in church just yesterday. I sat on her bed and sobbed, as it hit me that I'd never see her again and that it was all horribly unfair.

Toward evening, a car pulled into the driveway. Russell and I assumed it was Elizabeth, but instead it turned out to be Sam. He wore dark clothes, a dark hat, and dark glasses. I wondered idly if it was the same hat he'd worn the night before. It was apparent that Sam was feeling more relaxed than we did, and he even seemed to be happy about something. He leaned out of the open window and said he was just checking on us and couldn't stay long.

We walked over to Sam's car and I demanded angrily, "What happened last night? Why didn't the garlic protect Sierra?"

"I don't know," he said with a casual shrug that suggested he didn't really care. "Sometimes that happens. It's just like the shutters and door on this house. Sometimes their blue color protects you from ghosts and spirits, and sometimes it doesn't."

"Oh shit," Russell said. "That's why the houses around here all have blue shutters and doors?" He looked at me. "We've got to get the hell out of here."

To my surprise, Sam agreed. "That might not be a bad idea," he said, "now that we've found Big Jack's book."

"The song said Big Jack had a book, but Elizabeth thought it was treasure," I said. "Did you know it was really a book?"

"I had an idea it might be," he answered secretively, looking at me intently like a cat that was about to pounce.

"Well, are we going to get a chance to look at it?" I asked.

"We have to take it slow," he said and gave me a patronizing pat on the arm. "That book is old, and we don't want to damage it by moving too fast."

I was beginning to hate him. He'd dragged us off to hunt for Big Jack's treasure or book or whatever the hell it was, and now that he'd found it, he was ready to get rid of us. I didn't see any signs that he cared about Sierra's death.

"Elizabeth is filing a missing-person report on Sierra," I said, thinking I might scare him a little.

"Oh, really? The magistrate is a friend of mine," he said airily.

"You don't think he'll have questions about what happened to her?"

"Maybe," he said with a shrug. "I can explain what happened." He started the engine and began backing down the driveway. "Tell Elizabeth I'll be back tomorrow, will you?"

Still exhausted from the night before, I went to bed early, before Elizabeth had returned. Sam could explain what had happened to Sierra? How? Would he really tell the magistrate, "Snakes erupted from her skin and killed her"? I didn't believe that. He'd probably lie. And that lie could implicate Elizabeth, Russell, and me.

I really didn't trust him. I tossed in the bed, thinking about Sam and wondering why he seemed familiar to me. There was something about him...then I had an idea. It represented a dreadful possibility, but I *had* to look into it. Hopefully I was wrong.

I got up and looked through the pile of anthropology books I'd brought with me. One of them had a section on voodoo. I paged through it: voodoo was one of the religions developed by West African slaves in the Americas...voodoo contained elements of Christianity... voodoo was based on African beliefs that probably predated the Christian religion. I was getting close to what I was looking for but still hadn't found it.

Here was something: In voodoo, spirits called "loas" acted as intermediaries between God and people. Each loa had a distinctive look and area of specialty. Was that the memory that was bothering me?

I paged through photographs and drawings...and then, there it was...a drawing of a tall, thin Black man in a top hat and dark glasses. The caption was this:

> *Baron Samedi is one of the spirits or loas of Haitian voo-*
> *doo. He is usually depicted with a top hat, black tuxedo, dark*
> *glasses, and cotton plugs in his nostrils. He has a white, fre-*
> *quently skull-like face (or actually has a skull for a face), and*
> *speaks in a nasal voice.*

The all-powerful master of the dead, he can usually be found at the crossroads between the worlds of the living and the dead. He is associated with tools like spades and picks. When someone dies, he digs their grave and greets their soul after they have been buried, leading them to the underworld.

I shivered, and my stomach clutched with excitement, but also fear. Could Sam Dent be Baron Samedi? Was that possible? Sam's face was dark brown, not skull-like, but otherwise he came close. He was tall and thin, he wore a hat and dark glasses, and he lived near a graveyard.

Were the spirits that terrorized us in the graveyard under his control? He was the only member of our group whom they hadn't attacked. What had he said about them? *"They know me because I live among them."* At the time, I thought Sam was just referring to living near a graveyard. Now his words took on an entirely new meaning, one that I didn't like.

And if Sam Dent was Baron Samedi, what did that mean exactly? Was my tired mind just making things up? After all, lots of men wore dark suits, hats, and sunglasses; that didn't make them voodoo spirits. Should I ask Elizabeth about this? Where was she anyway?

My head spinning with questions, I gradually became aware of a strange rustling noise outside. It sounded like leaves blowing in the wind, even though there was almost no breeze. I parted the curtains in my bedroom and looked out—the night was quiet, and I didn't see anything moving. Yet the sound grew louder. Now it began to sound like wings, dozens of small wings. I heard something hitting the windows and ran into the living room just as Russell sprinted in from his bedroom.

"What the hell is going on?" he asked wildly, looking right and left.

"It sounds like birds or bats," I said. "We've got to close all the windows."

We rushed from room to room, slamming the screenless windows shut. We weren't fast enough, though, and I was horrified to see giant roaches spreading through the house. Some flew past my face. Others crawled on the windowsills or scurried across the floor. Screaming, I grabbed a shoe and began frantically killing them.

I heard Russell smashing them in another room and cheering himself on. "Got you, goddamn it! Got another one!"

While we were fighting the invasion, there were rapid steps outside, and the front door crashed open. Elizabeth ran into the living room, her face contorted.

"Russell! Finch!" she screamed. "Help me!" Horribly, she was covered with roaches that were burrowing into her hair and clinging to her clothes. We slapped them off her as quickly as we could and smashed them with our feet.

For a while, all we did was kill the giant roaches that streamed into the house. Then, as suddenly as it had started, the onslaught was over. It was silent inside and out, and we collapsed on the living room chairs.

"I'm sleeping *here* tonight," Russell said, and I decided to sleep in one of the chairs too. It was uncomfortable, but I felt more secure. There was definitely safety in numbers.

33

Elizabeth

June 13

I slept late Monday morning but still felt like hell when I finally forced myself out of bed. My head hurt, my legs ached, and my ears still rang slightly. The stinking clothes I'd thrown on a chair reawakened disgusting, vivid memories of our experiences at Big Jack's cabin. The ghostly voices and horrible smells...my fear of getting killed...I never wanted to go through something like that again. *But yet!* It had led us to the book of secrets, so I had to admit that it had all been worthwhile.

Except for Sierra...my thoughts swirled and my heart sank as I remembered her agonized death. Sierra had been the unwitting sacrifice in our quest for the book. Was that something Sam engineered? That was just one of my questions for him, along with *When are you giving me the book?*

I dragged myself to the back porch to wash up. Afterward I drove to the house of a local acquaintance and called him. The kids only knew about Mrs. Taylor's phone. I had additional options.

"Hey, Sam, it's me."

"Hi, babe. That was quite a night we had, wasn't it? How are you feeling?" Unlike the rest of us, he seemed to have been energized by our little adventure.

"Not that great." I got to the point. "Listen, can I come by today? I'd like to take a look at the book."

"Babe, I know you're eager to get started, but I think you should file a report on Sierra first." *Me? He was the one who knew the local system.*

"You want me to do it? I don't even know where to go."

"I'll tell you everything you need to know. It will probably take most of the afternoon, but you need to get started."

"You know the locals better than I do," I protested. "Why can't you do it?"

"She was a member of your team, wasn't she? She was your responsibility." I couldn't argue with his logic, but I still felt rebuffed, as though once again he was trying to block me from the book of secrets.

That afternoon, I drove to the magistrate's office, where Sam told me missing-person reports were filed. Not surprisingly, Russell and Finch were unhappy about Sierra and ready to call it quits, so I was glad to have an excuse to get away from the depressing atmosphere at the house.

The magistrate's office was in St. Pierre's courthouse, a shabby Greek revival survivor of the nineteenth century located in the island's largest town. The streets were hot, quiet, and felt like they were stuck in the 1950s. The magistrate's office was the same way. Behind the counter, a stuffy middle-aged white woman who was sitting at a computer rose slowly and reluctantly when I told her I needed assistance.

"What's your problem?" she asked in an unhelpful tone.

"I came to report a missing person," I explained. Sam and I agreed that this was a better approach than reporting Sierra's death. If we told the authorities that she'd died, they would ask for details that neither of us was prepared to provide. Better to keep it simple and not entirely inaccurate; she *was* missing, after all.

"When did this person go missing?"

"Last night."

"Last night? Are you sure she just ain't out partyin'? You know how y'all folks like to party." She laughed at her joke and glanced at me with her faded blue eyes like she thought I'd join in.

I chose not to react—her comment aptly reflected the primitive state of local race relations—and soldiered on. "No, I'm certain she's missing. She's a very responsible member of my research team, and she didn't come home last night. I'm sure something has happened to her."

"Research team? Are you that teacher from up North who's asking people about songs and such?"

My, how word travels on a small island, I thought. "Yes, that's me. I'm a *professor* of African American folklore at a university in Chicago." I emphasized professor and didn't smile, wanting the correction to sink in.

Without acknowledging it, the clerk continued. "You hang out with Sam Dent sometimes?"

Jesus, even this woman knows my business? "Yes," I said starchily, "he's been helping me with my research."

"He's a real character, ain't he?" she said casually. Now she had my attention.

"I suppose so…how do you mean?"

"Well, he showed up here about ten years ago and moved into that deserted house in the graveyard. Who wants to live in a graveyard? Somebody told me it might have belonged to his father, or somebody in his family; I don't know. Anyway, ever since he got here, he's been asking about the old-time Geechee stories, just like you."

"Really? I didn't know his interest went back that far." I kept my tone neutral, but I could feel my face getting hot. My heart pounded nervously. What the hell was going on with Sam?

She chattered on. "He's kind of an outsider here, like you. Maybe that's why you get along," she added with a sly little smile that I didn't like.

Time to get her out of my personal life. "If you can you give me the paperwork to fill out for the missing-person report, I'll let you get back to your work," I said briskly.

"Yes, ma'am," she said compliantly, returning to her desk to retrieve the forms.

When I returned the completed form to the clerk, she informed me that the magistrate's office normally waited three days before beginning an official inquiry. "Somebody from the office will be in touch," she assured me with a practiced smile.

I was about to leave when it occurred to me that perhaps I could conduct some additional research at the courthouse.

"Excuse me…"

"Ma'am?" The clerk looked up from her desk without returning to the counter.

"Is there an office here where I can check land records?"

"Sure, it's the second door on the right at the top of the stairs."

I wasn't sure what I was looking for, but I thought I'd start with the records for Sam's house in the graveyard. For instance, when exactly did he move in? Everyone said it was ten years ago, but what was the actual time period? The records might also show where he'd been living at the time of the sale and might even identify the seller.

The first step was finding the deed. Some counties had digitized records, but I quickly learned that St. Pierre still used paper files. Sighing, I resigned myself to a slow search.

Two hours and endless handwritten pages later, the records confirmed that a Samuel Dent held the deed to the house in the graveyard. But, confusingly, the deed was dated 1910, long before Sam was born. There was no record of subsequent transactions.

I reasoned that Sam might have inherited the property from a grandfather with whom he shared a name. It could have been an informal handoff that didn't involve official paperwork. Perhaps tax records would shed more light on the situation.

I walked over to that office and poured through more handwritten files. They verified that for the past ten years Samuel Dent, at his current address, had paid the property taxes on the land. Before then, and going back all the way to 1910, someone also named Samuel Dent had paid the taxes, but *that* person or *those* people—Sam's father and grandfather?—had lived on St. Pierre only until the 1920s. After that, the taxes were paid by check and were apparently sent by mail.

There might be a mystery there, or there might not. Clearly, more research was needed.

Just as I pondered my next move, another one of the middle-aged white clerks who populated the building tapped me on the shoulder and whispered that the office was about to close. Damn! I was going to have to come back on another day.

I wanted to swing past Sam's house, but the sun was setting, and there was no way I wanted to risk another trip through the graveyard. Before leaving the courthouse, I called him, but there was no answer. Since it looked like we'd be staying on St. Pierre for a while—or at least until I got possession of the book—I gave up on trying to track him down and drove to a neighboring island to pick up some food and supplies.

On the way there and back, I meditated on the clerk's comments about Sam. If he'd been asking questions about local folklore for years, when did he hear about the book of secrets? He'd been very smooth when I first told him about the book and mentioned my theory about it, but had he been too smooth? When he offered to help me, was it possible that I was really helping *him*? My mind churned with questions, and my suspicions grew. I decided to confront Sam about the book as soon as I could.

Having a plan made me feel a little better about the situation— but my tranquility was short lived. Pulling into the driveway, I heard a strange whirring sound that was almost like birds' wings, except that birds don't normally fly at night. Suddenly, the car was surrounded by clouds of flying roaches with long brown wings that glinted in the moonlight. They flew wildly, crisscrossing around me and blocking my path to the house. I left the groceries in the car and ran through the swirling mass, grimacing as the hard, dry bodies grazed my face, screaming and striking out as some clung to my clothing and crawled toward my face.

I staggered up the stairs and into the front room, where, to my horror, Russell and Finch were also battling the invading swarm. They slapped them off me, and together we trampled and killed the seemingly endless attackers. Finally, the onslaught was over. In the strange silence that followed our furious efforts, we collapsed in exhaustion on the creaky living room chairs and slept there through the night.

34

Finch
June 14

"What do we do now?" Russell asked Elizabeth over breakfast. It was another hot morning, and the air was ominously still, as though there might be a storm later. I'd heard that the storms on St. Pierre were violent and dangerous, and I dreaded the idea that one could be coming.

The three of us were sitting at the table on the little screened-in back porch. I looked over at Sierra's empty chair and felt guilty and sad. Elizabeth didn't answer Russell or meet our eyes.

"We collected your song for you," he went on, "and then we found Big Jack's treasure that turned out to be a book. What more do you want? Do we have to wait here until they find Sierra?"

"I want you to keep working," Elizabeth said flatly.

"What?" Russell and I said together.

"Are you serious? Working on what?" I added.

"Yes, we've had a setback," she said. "But before we go, I think we can find out more about Big Jack. I just have a feeling about that."

"So losing Sierra was just a setback? That's how you feel? Just a setback? What more is there to find out about Big Jack?" I asked, furiously. "He had a treasure that was by the water. It turned out to be a book, and now we've found it. Just ask Sam if you can look at it, and then we're through. You can write an article about it and be famous," I finished sarcastically.

"I'm not sure it's that simple," Elizabeth replied in the same flat tone.

"What's that supposed to mean?" I asked. Again, she didn't answer. I was suddenly sick of both them—her and Sam. I didn't care about the song, and I didn't care about the book. I just wanted to get to the bottom of Sierra's death and get the hell out of St. Pierre. Were Russell and I the only ones who cared about how and why she died?

"Don't you care about how Sierra died?" I screamed at Elizabeth.

"I don't understand what happened any more than you do," she hedged.

"Well, can't you find out? What was all that craziness about? Was that real? Where did it come from? Why are you obsessing about Big Jack instead?"

"If we find out more about Big Jack, maybe we'll answer those questions too."

Please. It was all too smooth. I went in my room, slamming the door so hard that the tiny house shook. *Maybe this one will fall down too,* I thought angrily.

That afternoon, Elizabeth took us to a little cluster of houses on one of the sandy roads so that we could continue our research on the Big Jack song.

"What do you want us to ask about?" Russell asked sullenly.

"I want you to find out if the verses we know are the same ones other people tell you about. Maybe it starts a different way than what we think. Maybe there are more verses than the ones we've heard. The only way to find out is to keep asking people," she answered edgily. "Come on, use your brains," she added, as though we were trying to slack off.

She put the car in gear and said, "I'll meet you back here about four p.m."

"You're not coming with us?" Russell asked sharply. "Where are *you* going?"

"I have to follow up with the magistrate about Sierra." That sounded reasonable, and as though Elizabeth cared. Maybe I didn't completely despise her.

"Just get back before the storm comes," Russell said over his shoulder as he got out of the car. We started trudging down the road under the ferocious sun.

That afternoon I learned that there *was* more to the Big Jack song. Frighteningly more. And I wondered how much Elizabeth had known all along.

The turning point was an elderly woman who lived in the third house I stopped at.

Russell and I had separated so that we could talk to more people. Perspiring from the beating sun and listening to the sand crunching under my shoes, I spotted a small house by itself in a field of lush plants whose rich smell signaled ripening tomatoes. It was an inviting aroma, and I decided to stop. As usual, I worried about dogs—vicious, snarling packs had driven me away from many houses on St. Pierre—but today I was lucky.

As I got closer, I saw a woman sitting on the doorstep. I could tell from her posture and features that she was elderly, but her skin was smooth and almost unwrinkled. Its dark-brown tone contrasted richly with the white scarf tied around her hair. She was smoking a little pipe. I thought I recognized her from church.

"Good morning, ma'am," I said politely. "I mean, good afternoon." She looked at me and nodded.

"I think I saw you in church last Sunday. May I sit down?" She silently nodded again and exhaled some smoke.

"My name is Finch," I said. "I'm one of the students that the pastor introduced. Do you remember that?" Another nod. "We're doing research on old-time songs and stories and things like that."

"My name is Massie," she answered in a low but strong voice. "They call me Miss Massie. Which songs?" I was so surprised to hear her question that I jumped a little.

"Beg your pardon?"

"Which songs, child?"

"Oh, uh, Big Jack. That's the one we're working on now. Do you know that one?"

"I know it," she said simply, and frowned. "Why that one?"

No one had asked me that question before—and I realized suddenly that I didn't know the answer to it.

"It's the one our professor asked us to find out more about," I said sheepishly. I felt stupid and used. Why was I just going along with Elizabeth's program?

Massie exhaled again and looked out over the tomato field. "It's not a good song," she said quietly.

What? "Why is that?" I asked. She looked out over the field, and for a long moment, I thought she wasn't going to answer.

"The song makes people do foolish things. They want what's in Big Jack's book, but it's not for them. There's a reason the book was hidden." Chills ran up and down my spine.

Massie looked directly into my eyes with her own, which were small and bright.

"I hear Big Jack's book a-been found now."

My heart pounded. "How-how do you know?" I said, stuttering.

"There are signs," she said. "Some of us know these things."

My stomach twisted into knots, and I wanted to run away, even though I didn't know what I was running from. Massie looked at me again and held my attention with her steady gaze. She exhaled; I smelled the fragrant perfume of her tobacco. Another long moment passed.

"That professor"—she almost spat the word—"of yours is very stupid. She has put you in big danger. Big Jack's secrets are for him alone, but now it's too late."

My chest shook from the pounding of my heart. "What? Why?" I said, "I don't understand."

"Listen to the song, and you will," she answered simply.

Massie put down her pipe and began to sing in her low-pitched voice. The tune was melancholy, almost spooky, just like when Sam sang it, but there were more verses now, verses he hadn't sung.

Big Jack had a secret book
He did; yes, he did
He kept it by his side
He did; yes, he did
He lived beside the water
He did; yes, he did
Where the salt marsh meets the tide
He did; yes, he did
Massa murdered Big Jack
He did; yes, he did
For wanting to be free
He did; yes, he did
He cut him into pieces,
Yes, he did; yes, he did
And threw him in the sea
Yes, he did; yes, he did
Don't trouble Big Jack's secrets
Keep away; keep away
Don't try to read his book
Shut your eyes; shut your eyes
It's a book of fearsome power
Stay away! Stay away!
You'll be cursed if you look
Stay away! Stay away!

After "stay away" she looked at me again, straight in the eyes.

"Listen to the song, Finch. Big Jack's book is cursed. People shouldn't have anything to do with it. But it's too late now, and there's no turning back!" She was almost shouting and there was fear in her eyes.

I jumped up so quickly that I nearly fell backward. The next thing I knew, I was running through the field, squashing nearly ripe tomatoes in my panic, and recklessly running away from the knowledge I didn't want to have. The air was so thick and heavy that I could barely breathe. Once again, instinct told me that Russell and I had to get off this island—or was it too late for us too?

35

Finch

June 14

Out of breath, sweating, sticky, upset, I ran most of the way down the road to the place where Elizabeth, Russell, and I had agreed to meet. There was no one there. I checked my watch. It was three p.m.—an hour to go before Elizabeth was due. There was nothing for me to do but to try to collect myself.

I was frightened for my safety and furious with Elizabeth. Now I had confirmation that she'd taken advantage of us. Why had she done it? I didn't know. But in any event, I'd had enough. Maybe the Big Jack song was only that, a song, just a song—despite its message of warning—but when I added what Miss Massie said to everything else that had happened, the signs weren't good. Maybe Russell and I could find a way to get away…that very night if possible.

I settled down under one of the large oaks to wait for him. The air was getting heavier, if that was possible. My thoughts churned with what I'd heard from Miss Massie. *There's a reason it was hidden… She has put you in big danger…Big Jack's secrets are for him alone, but now it's too late.* What kind of danger was she talking about? What could happen to us?

I noticed that around me the leaves were turning their silver undersides upward. My grandmother always said this was a sure sign of rain. As if to confirm my thoughts, thunder rumbled distantly. The sky was unusually dark, and I noticed that the animals and insects that normally filled the air with their chirping, croaking, and other sounds had fallen silent.

I looked at my watch again. It was three thirty. Where the hell was Russell? I spotted a man walking along the side of the road and got to my feet.

"Russell!" I called out, "Hurry up; I have something to tell you!"

There was no response, and the man kept his head down. Perhaps Russell hadn't heard me.

I ran closer and called again, "Russell!"

This time, the man raised his head, and I saw his contorted dark face and twisted mouth. As I started to scream, I looked down...no feet! Terrified, I tripped, fell, and scrambled up as quickly as I could, running back toward the tree where I'd been waiting for Russell and Elizabeth.

The tree was near the junction of the main road and the sandy road Miss Massie lived on, and it was a logical place to meet. But now my heart sank when I remembered that ghosts—and the devil—were said to populate crossroads. Was I safe? Were more of them coming? I fingered the garlic pendant that I still wore around my neck, hoping it would protect me.

Thunder rumbled again, much closer now. Terrified that the ghost had followed me to the tree, I held on to the garlic for dear life and went into a fetal curl with my eyes squeezed tightly shut. The wind and thunder intensified and rain began pelting the tree. The peals of thunder were so loud that it seemed they would shatter the sky into pieces. I had never felt so alone.

When I felt a touch on my shoulder, I panicked, screaming and rushing to my feet. I was certain that the ghost I'd seen was preparing to attack. Clearly, Sam's garlic necklace was powerless to protect me. Maybe it only worked when he was around. *Except that it hadn't for Sierra.*

To my tremendous relief, it was Russell who was touching me, not the ghost. He was soaked and looked as frightened as I felt. Impulsively, I hugged him tightly.

"Are you okay?" he shouted in my ear.

"Russell, I have something to tell you!" I shouted back. "We're not safe here. We have to get away!" He looked at me quizzically, but I couldn't explain just then because of the escalating storm.

The storm raged around us, and we sheltered under the massive oak, fearful of both natural dangers, like flying branches, and unnatural ones, like the wandering ghosts.

The man I'd seen on the road had disappeared, thank God, but suspicious foggy shapes sometimes floated before our eyes and then blew away in the wind like handkerchiefs. The thunder was so intense that at times the tree shook down to its roots.

At first we couldn't talk, but as the storm wound down, I told Russell what I'd heard from Miss Massie. "Son of a bitch!" he shouted when I'd finished. "What the fuck is going on? And where is Elizabeth? Did she forget about us?"

Finally, when it was closer to five p.m., we saw a vehicle coming toward us. The thunder and wind were long gone, and leftover raindrops pattered on the ground around us. The world was more peaceful, although broken branches on the road bore witness to the fury of the earlier storm.

The vehicle wasn't Elizabeth's car, though, but a truck. As it came closer, I saw it was Sam's. To my surprise, Elizabeth was sitting in the passenger's seat.

"Hey, you two," she called out, as though it were an ordinary afternoon. "Sorry I'm a bit late. I had car problems, and I asked Sam Dent for a lift."

Sam leaned across her and shouted, "Climb on into the back. You won't get any wetter than you are already."

Ha-ha. Climbing over the side brought back sickening memories of our misadventures on Sunday night. I didn't want to be in the back of Sam's truck again.

We bumped and swerved back to the house, with Sam's truck dodging branches and puddles in the road. When he pulled into the driveway, there was no sign of Elizabeth's car, and I wondered where she'd left it. Maybe it was at his house.

Getting down from the back, I spotted something lying on the floor of the truck. On a whim, I picked it up and put it in my pocket. There were broken tree limbs in the sandy driveway, and patches of moss torn from the trees lay everywhere. Russell went in the house first, and I followed behind. Fortunately, the power was on.

When I turned to see if Elizabeth was following behind us, I saw her touching Sam affectionately and whispering something in his ear. So that embrace I'd seen at Sally's Club wasn't a fluke. I wondered what the nature of Elizabeth's relationship with Sam really was. How much wasn't she telling us?

Ugh. I was confused and tired and just wanted to get to bed. I didn't even want to eat.

Undressing, I took the object from my pocket that I'd found in the truck. It was a garlic pendant on a yellow cord. It was Sierra's pendant—which meant she wasn't wearing it when we went to Big Jack's cabin. That was odd, considering Sam had tied it around her neck just before we got in the truck. What had happened?

36

Elizabeth
June 14

This afternoon, I dropped Russell and Finch off near one of the backwoods communities and told them I was going to follow up with the local magistrate about Sierra's death. It was one of those sections of St. Pierre that don't seem to have changed since the nineteenth century—it's amazing. Anyway, I knew they'd be busy for several hours, which would give me time to conduct some private business with Sam. I certainly never imagined they'd find out about the rest of Big Jack's song that day.

Sam *knows* that Big Jack's book of secrets is rightfully mine! It was my idea from the beginning to look for it, ever since I pieced together the verses of Big Jack's song during my first trips to St. Pierre. I'd been hoping to find it for years. Then Sam offered to help me and told me to bring a team of students on my next research trip. I could tell them the song was about treasure; there was no need for them to know the full story. Okay, I went along with his plan. But then, God damn him, he betrayed me. I thought I could trust him, and he took the book—*my* book!

Prepared to do whatever was necessary to get it back, I drove to the graveyard, parked on the road, and followed one of the paths through the gravestones to Sam's house. At night, I would need his protection from the spirits that lived here, but in the daytime I felt safe.

Sam's house was an old one built of wood and oyster shells. It resembled Big Jack's cabin and might have been almost as old. The windows were cloudy with age, and strips of peeling blue paint dangled from the shutters and wood trimming. He must have seen me coming through one of those cloudy windows, because he opened the door before I'd even knocked.

He greeted me with "To what do I owe the pleasure, Elizabeth?" as if he didn't know.

"I just want to talk about the book of secrets," I replied. "Can't we be reasonable, Sam? You know it was my idea to look for it, and now you're keeping it from me."

"Keeping it from you?" he said with a sly smile. "Aren't you being a little paranoid, babe? Don't you trust me? You know I'm as interested in the book of secrets as you are. I just need some time to study it."

I wasn't buying that story, and he knew it. I walked past him into the house and paced nervously around his small, dimly lit front room.

"How do you see in here?" I complained. "It's so dark I can barely see."

"I have all the light I need," he laughed. "You're so anxious, Elizabeth. Can I get you a beer?"

While he was in the kitchen, I perused a number of faded photographs that were lined up on his mantel in gilt frames. One showed what looked like Sam as a small boy. Dressed in a smart little shorts suit and wearing a small cap, he was seated on the knee of a slim, dark-skinned man in a suit with an old-fashioned cut. Next to them stood a lighter complexioned woman who wore a beautifully ruffled dress in the style of the early nineteen hundreds. Her long dark hair was gathered under an enormous feathered hat.

"Sam," I called out, "is the little boy in this photograph your father?"

"Which one?"

"The one of the fashionable little boy with the two adults."

"Ha," he laughed. "No, that's me."

"You're joking, right?" I said incredulously. "That's impossible! Based on how the people are dressed, that picture is at least a hundred years old. That would make you how old?"

Sam walked in the room with our beers, winked by way of a response, and said, "It's a mystery, isn't it? But you like a mystery." He had always been secretive about his background, and I hated it. But I knew I wouldn't get anywhere by asking questions—I'd tried that before—so I dropped the subject.

Ironically, as secretive as he was about himself, he'd also been helpful with my research. We'd first met when he overheard me at Mrs. Taylor's store asking questions about local folklore. He'd followed me out to my car and said reassuringly, "Don't take it personally if you don't get far with your questions. Folks on St. Pierre can be pretty suspicious of outsiders. Maybe I can help. I was once an outsider here myself."

And now here we were. We'd found what we'd been looking for, but now he didn't want to play fair.

I stared at him across my beer and frowned. He smoothed my forehead with his finger. "Don't look so worried, Elizabeth. You'll see the book, I promise."

"When?" I urged.

"Always so impatient!" he replied. He leaned across the table where we were sitting and kissed me. One thing led to another and, like so many times before, we ended up on his old, velvet couch, where we had the slow, intense sex that I enjoyed so much with him.

He was slim, muscular, well endowed, and not afraid to take his time. He had the energy of a young man and the lovemaking skills of a mature one. It was delightful, and I never wanted it to end.

By the time we finished, I was covered with perspiration from the hot air of the room and the body heat we'd generated.

"Look at me," I murmured into Sam's ear. "Do I look like someone who's been talking to a magistrate?"

"You can just tell the kids it was a heated discussion," Sam laughed, leaning down to kiss one of my breasts.

When we came up for air again, it was so dark that I thought it was actually night.

"What time is it?" I asked Sam sleepily.

He looked at his watch and said, "It's a little after three."

"Good; that means we still have time. But why is it so dark outside?"

"There must be a storm coming." He walked to the window, which gave me a chance to admire the lines of his fine body.

"Yes, it's going to be a bad one," he said, looking at me over his shoulder. He headed back toward the couch. "Are you worried about the kids?"

I pulled him down on top of me. "They'll be okay," I assured him.

The storm arrived minutes later and crashed around us. Thunder occasionally shook the house, and rain pelted the ancient windows so hard that some of it came inside. It splashed refreshingly against my skin as I straddled Sam and felt him deep inside me.

Just after he climaxed with a loud groan, I started my campaign. We were lying together, damp and lazy, our hearts thumping.

"Sam," I whispered, "can I see the book before I leave?"

"You never give up, do you?"

"No, I never do."

Without answering my question, he got up and walked into the bathroom where—unlike our house—there was running water. "Isn't it time for you to go?" he called out.

I looked at my watch. "Shit! I'm late."

I washed up quickly and pulled my clothes back on. Outdoors, the air was refreshing, although branches were scattered everywhere from the storm. I retraced my steps to my car, glad that it wasn't dark yet.

The engine didn't respond. I tried again, listening to it grind over and over without catching. Finally, I gave up and walked back down the path to Sam's. Out of the corner of my eye, I thought I saw something moving under the trees, so I hurried.

"Well, if it isn't you again," he greeted me. "You couldn't get enough?"

I laughed. "My car won't start. I need a ride from you so that I can pick up the kids."

"That's no problem," he said agreeably, and I wondered if maybe I was making progress.

The question was: Was he playing into my hands or was I playing into his?

37

Finch

June 15

At breakfast, I told Elizabeth about my conversation with Miss Massie and the missing verses of the song. She didn't show any reaction, so I pushed—more than I would have just a few weeks ago. Our relationship was changing; I wondered if she was aware of it too.

"The song says 'stay away,'" I said, looking at her hard, "and it says that the book is cursed. Miss Massie said that finding it was dangerous. So what are we doing? Shouldn't we just leave the book alone?"

I gave Elizabeth another steady look and was disgusted that she couldn't even meet my eye. She drank some coffee and glanced away.

"The woman said that Big Jack's secrets are his alone. And she said it might be too late." Now Elizabeth rolled her eyes and laughed at me dismissively.

"Too late for what? You can't listen to everything these old people around here say."

With that provocation, my anger boiled over. "What? I thought these people here were the authorities. Now it's all just mumbo jumbo?"

I looked over to Russell for moral support, but he was looking at his plate. He sometimes challenged Elizabeth, but fundamentally he disliked confrontation. That meant that I was on my own again.

"Oh, come on, Finch, take it easy," Elizabeth said, looking my way with a kind of half-assed smile. "We know that these people aren't that well educated. They have a lot of beliefs that are just...superstitions. All this talk about Big Jack's book being dangerous is just that: it's talk. The book has been lost for a long time. No one knows what's in it."

"The local people are ignorant now? What happened to your respect for their folk knowledge and the African tradition?" She was so full of shit; I just wanted to be finished with her.

"If Big Jack's book isn't dangerous, what happened to us in the cabin?" I continued. "Look how Sierra died. Was that just superstitions? No, it was crazy—and it was *real*! If we'd stayed away, like the song says, she'd still be alive now."

"I didn't even know it was a book until the other night," she said defensively. "I thought it was a treasure. But I was wrong, wasn't I? And...and I don't understand the things that happened to Sierra either."

At that moment, it seemed like she genuinely cared about Sierra's death.

"Finch, now we need to find out what's in the book. We don't need to be afraid of it; we need to learn more about it. Maybe it will help us understand about Sierra." She gave that strange, shifty look of hers again, along with another half-assed smile.

But what she said kind of made sense, and I felt a little silly. Maybe I *had* been overreacting.

"How are we going to do that when Sam has the book?" I asked sulkily.

"You're exactly right," she answered.

"When I get my car from his house, I'm going to look at the book too." She stood up. "In fact, I think I'll call him now from Taylor's store and ask him to pick me up. While I'm gone, can you and Russell enter our field notes into the computer?"

That afternoon, Russell and I sat on the front porch, dutifully sifting through our notes and occasionally waving at cars that drove by.

We were careful when it came to pedestrians. First, we had to make sure they had feet; luckily, they all did.

It looked like I was working on my notes, but in fact I was having trouble concentrating. First of all, I was concerned about Sierra. Elizabeth hadn't said anything about her before she left. Was the magistrate going to take action? Could we be charged with her death? When did Elizabeth plan to notify her parents?

Second, what was the deal with Elizabeth's car? Now it was at Sam's house apparently. But yesterday she had said that she'd broken down *somewhere* and didn't say anything about his house. Did she have her car towed to Sam's? Was I thinking about this too much?

Finally, I wondered again whether I could make sense of what was happening to us on St. Pierre. Did I really believe that ghosts roamed up and down the road? What about the events at Big Jack's cabin? They felt real, but were they? Could I possibly have imagined them? But we had all heard the same sounds and seen the same horrible things that happened to Sierra. Could that mean there was a different reality here on St. Pierre? A world I'd never known about before?

Or was the truth that I—or we—had been manipulated into experiencing things that weren't possible? If that was the case, was Sam behind it all like some kind of evil mastermind? Not Sam as Baron Samedi, but just someone who for his own, still unknown, purposes was trying to convince us that the supernatural was real?

Questions! My mind churned with them. It was all very confusing, and I didn't know where to turn for answers.

I stopped pretending to work and said, "Russell, what do you want to do?" He looked up from his computer.

"Do about what?"

"About our situation. Do you want to stay, or should we try to leave? Aren't you worried about all the stuff that's been going on?"

He thought about it for a minute. "I kind of want to stay," he said slowly. "I guess I want to find out more about the book. I mean, we've already put in all this work"—he waved at our notebooks and computer—"and we might as well see what it adds up to."

That made sense in a way. "And I have my garlic," he said with a little laugh.

I decided to share some of my anxieties. "What do you think about what happened to us in the graveyard and at Big Jack's cabin? Do you think those things were real? You know, the spirits we saw, and the sounds we heard, and, uh, the snakes and Sierra?" I still preferred euphemisms to acknowledging that she was dead.

He shook his head. "I don't know what to think about it. I guess I've tried not to in a way. I mean, I know what I think I saw, but it was nighttime...maybe we were hallucinating or something. Anyway, I'm pretty sure the box and the book that Sam found are real; they looked pretty solid. And I suppose we could always go back to that island to see whether there's anything there that matches what we remember."

That reminded me of my discovery from the night before. I went into my bedroom and brought out Sierra's garlic on its yellow cord and dangled it from my finger. "Look at what I found in the back of the truck," I announced. Russell stared without recognition, so I helped him. "It's the amulet Sam gave Sierra on Sunday night!"

"Whoa...does that mean she didn't have it when we found the book and when that, uh, stuff happened to her?" Russell was more comfortable with euphemisms too.

"That's exactly what it means, and it's just another weird thing about that night. I guess Sam didn't tie it tightly enough around her neck, and it fell off."

Somewhere in the depths of my mind, another theory stirred and began to take shape, but I pushed it away; it was too ugly.

Elizabeth drove home later that afternoon. "The car seems to be fine," I said to her, peering from the porch to the driveway. "What was wrong with it?"

"Oh, it was something about the battery," she replied vaguely.

She looked over at Russell and said, "How are those notes coming?"

"We're finished," Russell answered. "What are we going to do next? Did you see the book? When do we get to see it?"

"Slow down, pardner," Elizabeth said with a half laugh. Her lips smiled, but her eyes didn't. "Sam knows that we want to look at it, but, well, he might need some persuading."

"What's that mean?" I asked. But she went into her room and didn't answer.

An hour later or so, Elizabeth and I were in the tiny, hot kitchen off the back porch, preparing dinner. I dropped a spoon on the ancient, cracked linoleum floor and just happened to glance at her legs as I got up. To my surprise, several large, dark-blue bruises were clearly visible under the medium brown of her skin.

"Elizabeth, what happened?" I asked, standing up quickly. She saw that I was looking at her legs.

"Oh"—a little shaky laugh—"Sam likes to play rough." She flushed and looked away. I was so shocked I was speechless.

After dinner, I cornered her while Russell cleaned up.

"Are you okay? Did Sam hurt you?" We didn't have a close relationship, but I needed to know. My protective instincts were raised—not a feeling I expected to have toward Elizabeth.

"Thanks," she said with another shaky laugh. "It's a little embarrassing, really. I-I didn't think you could see the marks. Like I said, he just likes it a little rough."

"A little rough?" I couldn't stop myself. "Have you seen those bruises? Are there more that I can't see?"

"Well at least he spared my face," she said and looked away. I was suddenly disgusted that she would defend him.

"Do you play rough too? Do you like it that way too?" I felt so confused. He could have hurt her. Did she need my help or not? Did I care?

"Look, Finch," Elizabeth said with a firmer tone, "I know what I'm doing. You don't have to worry about me."

"What are you doing?" I yelled. "Why are you getting involved with him? I don't get it. Let's just get Big Jack's book from him and get the hell away from this place."

"Maybe this *is* my way of getting the book," she said with a little smirk.

"Oh, please!" I shouted.

Russell came into the room with a dishtowel in his hand and a quizzical look on his face just as I turned and ran into my bedroom. I cried myself to sleep that night, thinking, *I don't understand what's going on. I just want to go home.*

38

June 15

Finch confronted me this morning about Big Jack's song. Thanks to
an old woman named Miss Massie, she heard all the verses, and now
she knows that the song ends with the warning to stay away.

I tried to convince her that it wasn't as bad as it sounds. I reminded
her that the people on St. Pierre are superstitious. Just because they
say something is cursed doesn't necessarily mean it really is. I also
reminded her that the book of secrets has been hidden for generations, so people today have no idea what's in it. My reasoning seemed
to work with her...I assume it reassured Russell too.

Of course, the true story is in the verses of Miss Massie's song—
but Finch and Russell don't need to know that. They only need to
know enough to be helpful to me.

Besides, what's a curse? To me, what the old-timers call a curse is
actually a form of power. You just have to know how to use it. That's
why I have to have the book. I know how to use the power, and Sam
doesn't. How can I trust him with the book of secrets when I don't
even know who he really is? That's why the book should be mine.

Yesterday, I tried to get the book from Sam and wasn't able to.
Today, I thought I might succeed. The first step was to get back to his
house. I called from the store and asked him to pick me up so that I

could get my car. Meanwhile, I instructed Russell and Finch to transfer their notes to their computers.

We drove silently to Sam's house. He could tell I wasn't in a talking mood. We pulled up by the graveyard and he said, "I got your car started, Elizabeth. I think something in the engine got wet in yesterday's storm." A pause. "Are you in a rush or do you have time to come in for a drink?"

I knew what "drink" implied and thought for a moment whether I would accept his offer. What other plan did I have for getting the book? No plan, really, if I was honest with myself. So I smiled and followed him into the house.

This time, things went downhill very quickly. It's hard to think about, but I have to write about it anyway.

We were drinking—whiskey on ice this time—and lying on his bed. The windows were open to let in the breeze, and I felt relaxed and trusting. Sam pushed me back softly and pulled off my clothes, then lay down between my legs and nuzzled my breasts.

I could feel heat rising from my skin, and my legs fell open more, ready to receive him. Sam gradually moved lower, and I thought he was going to lick me. Instead, he bit me hard on the thigh.

"Ouch!" I said. "That hurt!"

"I know," he said, looking up with a wicked smile. "A little pain helps the pleasure, in my book."

Then he bit me again. "Ouch!" I protested.

"Oh, come on now," he said, and moved up to kiss me. His hard cock pushed against my leg, and it was clear that the biting had turned him on. I'll put up with it, I thought, if it gets me what I want. *You're trading your body for a book,* a voice said in my head. *Have you no shame? No, it's more than a book,* another voice argued. *It's the book of secrets. It's worth it.*

Sam entered me, and soon our mutual pleasure silenced the warring voices. Our lovemaking—it was more than sex, wasn't it? Weren't we kind of in love?—was intense and overpowering. Later, we lay tangled together on the bed, catching our breath.

"Wow," I said after a while, "that was something else." I propped myself on one elbow and looked at him. "Sam..."

"Please, don't start with me," he protested. "Let's just enjoy the moment. Can't you see that there's something special between us?"

I ignored his question. "Sam, look, I'm going to have to leave St. Pierre soon, and I'm not leaving without the book." There, I'd said it. It was something I'd been thinking about all along, but I'd never said it to him before.

All of a sudden, his demeanor changed, and he glared at me like an animal. It was such a vicious look that I actually recoiled.

"God damn it," he shouted. "The book is mine. You're not getting it!"

"What are you saying?" I screamed back, jumping out of the bed. "The book of secrets belongs to me! I'm the one who discovered the song."

"I let you think you discovered it," he sneered, "but I'm the one who figured out that we needed Sierra to get the book."

His first statement threw me for a loop. What was he saying? If he'd always known about the song, why did he lead me to believe otherwise? What game was he playing with me? My confusion just made me angrier. "Go on and say it straight," I challenged. "You're the one who figured out that we had to kill Sierra to get the book of secrets."

"Well, you went along with it, didn't you?" he countered. "You lured her down here knowing she was going to die."

"Bullshit!" I responded. "I trusted you. You said to bring a team, and you never said why."

"What would you know about trust?" he hurled back. "When we were at Big Jack's cabin, you figured out that we were exchanging Sierra for the book. But you went along with it, didn't you? You didn't even try to save her. Sierra trusted *you*, and look how you repaid her."

"The book of secrets is worth it," I responded defensively. I felt bad about what had happened to Sierra—I truly did—but I also wanted that book *more than anything in the world.*

"I'm sorry she had to die, but I know the book is worth it," I repeated.

"You don't even know what's in it," he screamed.

"Not yet," I said, "but I will as soon as I get my hands on it."

Furiously, and still naked, I began rifling through the piles of books and clothes in his bedroom.

"I know it's in here *somewhere*. Where have you hidden it?" I moved feverishly through the room, flinging things into the air. "If it wasn't so goddamned dark in here, I could probably find it!" I raged.

Sam came up behind me, but I didn't hear him. The next thing I knew, he'd slammed me to the floor with a blow to my ribs.

I screamed and tried to get to my feet, but he held my shoulder down with one strong arm. Over and over, he punched me with the other hand, aiming his blows at my legs and torso, carefully avoiding my face.

"You coward!" I screamed, kicking out wildly and trying to dodge his blows. "You get off on hurting women, don't you? But you don't want to get found out, so you won't hit my face. You don't want anyone to know what a bastard you are."

He stopped hitting me and held me down by both shoulders.

"Just give me what I want, Elizabeth, and I'll give you the book." He was actually smiling, and he'd gotten hard again, the fucking sadist. "Come on, Elizabeth, nobody does it like we do. Just give me what I want. You know you like it too."

We did it right there on the dusty floor. I couldn't fool myself and call it lovemaking this time. Sam thrust into me, grunting low in his throat and oblivious to everything but his own satisfaction. Meanwhile, I lay there and absorbed the impact, with silent tears rolling down my cheeks into the dust. I was in pain from his blows, from the grinding of my shoulder blades and hipbones into the floor—and from the humiliation of what I was willing to do for the sake of the book of secrets.

After Sam had finished and lay sleeping, I scrambled out from under him and sat on the side of the bed. Already, I could see bruises forming on my thighs and ribcage. I could even see the outline of his teeth where he'd bitten me. Jesus, I was a mess! And I still didn't have the book. Should I look for it again while he slept?

I dressed quietly and began poking around in the corners of the room. This time, I was quieter than before, but I still had no idea where to look.

Sam stirred on the floor and opened his eyes. Maybe he'd only been pretending to be asleep.

"What are you doing, babe?" I heard the warning in his voice and wasn't fooled by the "babe."

"Nothing. I'm looking for the rest of my clothes. I'm getting ready to go."

"Okay," he said in a reasonable tone, "I'll walk you to your car."

Incredibly, he said this without irony, as though just an hour before he hadn't subjected me to uncontrolled physical and sexual violence. And that contrast—the solicitous tone after his previous rage, his gentlemanly manners after the viciousness of the afternoon—made me realize what a very dangerous man he was. To him, what he had done to me was okay; it was acceptable behavior.

We walked to my car, and I thought what a fool I'd been to think I could use sex to get the book of secrets from Sam—and what an idiot I was to believe his lies about giving it to me.

39

Finch

June 16

When I got up, the house was quiet. I felt dopey from crying myself to sleep, and my head ached. I trudged to the back porch and found Russell reading there, slurping a cup of coffee.

"Where's Elizabeth?"

"She left already. She said she was going to Sam's house."

I sniffed by way of a response and went down the steps to the outhouse. The red ants still tried to swarm up our legs when we crossed into their territory, but we'd all gotten adept at avoiding them.

After using the outhouse, I pumped some water into a bucket that I took into my room so that I could wash up. I'd gotten to be an old hand at functioning without running water.

I joined Russell on the back porch and quietly brooded about our trip to Big Jack's cabin. Images of Sierra's death haunted me. I thought that Russell probably felt the same way, even though we didn't talk about it. Elizabeth certainly didn't seem to be too bothered. She'd only mentioned Sierra a few times since that night.

Drinking a couple of cups of coffee helped me think more clearly, and I decided to visit Myma again. I hadn't seen her in a few days.

"Hey, Russell," I shouted, as I walked down the front steps. "I'm going to see Miss Myma. You're in charge." He laughed.

On a brilliant, hot day like this one, with a slight breeze and the sun glinting off the trees, St. Pierre felt more familiar and not as strange as it had before. It wasn't like home, but I could appreciate its beauty. It was so green and fertile, abundant with nature, yet also mysterious and secretive.

I looked up at an egret that was flying overhead. It landed in a tree along a nearby salt creek, its stunning white feathers sharply outlined against the dark-green foliage. Yes, today the island felt like a very special place.

Just as I turned into Myma's yard, a car honked. Caesar waved out of the window, and I briefly wondered where he was going. But I forgot about him as I greeted Myma.

She was seated as usual on the stoop outside her door, with the small clay pipe she liked to smoke in her hand.

"Hello, child. How are you today?" she asked warmly. I handed her some groceries that I'd brought as a gift and then took a seat next to her on a chair bottom that had four legs but no back.

I wanted to ask Myma about Sam Dent, but not right away. So I chatted about various things that had happened in the last few days. Finally, I got my courage up and said "Elizabeth has been spending a lot of time with Sam lately."

"I know," Myma replied. And then, to my shock, she added, "They are old friends."

"W-what?" I stuttered. "They knew each other before?"

"Long time," she said casually. "Long time Elizabeth has been coming here searching for Big Jack's book. And long time Sam has been searching for it too."

"But we only found out it was a book when we went to that little island," I protested. "When we came here, Elizabeth said we were looking for a treasure."

"Elizabeth says all kinds of things," Myma replied scornfully. "She says what she wants to get what she wants."

*Wonderful...*my headache started up again and the day didn't seem as beautiful as it had before.

"What's so special about this book?" I asked.

Myma puffed reflectively on her pipe and didn't answer right away. Then her dark eyes flicked toward me, and she said evasively, "It's a powerful book. It's the book of life and death—"

"I know," I interrupted. "That's what the song says, but what does that mean?"

"It's very powerful," she repeated, "and it should never have been disturbed. Now Elizabeth has put you in danger."

A chill went down my spine. "You knew that we found the book? How did you know?"

"There are signs," she answered. It was the same thing Miss Massie had said on the day of the storm. "There are signs, if you know how to read them...and I do."

Abruptly, she turned and looked directly into my eyes. "Be careful, Finch. Elizabeth will do anything to get what she wants. She wants the book, because she wants its power. She doesn't care about anyone or anything else, including you."

My thoughts swirled, and I felt surrounded by mysteries and shadows.

"Well, why did she bring us with her to search for the book if she wants it for herself? And why did she lie and call it a treasure?"

Myma puffed on her pipe again and narrowed her eyes thoughtfully. "Maybe she and Sam couldn't do it alone. Maybe they needed something or someone else..."

Suddenly, the dark thought that had been in the back of my mind sprang to life. "Maybe they needed a sacrifice of some kind?"

Myma looked at me sharply, and I told her about Sam's necklace that was supposed to have protected Sierra from harm.

"Miss Myma, what if it wasn't an accident that the necklace came off?" She pressed her lips together and didn't answer.

Then she looked at me again and said, "Be careful, my child. Protect yourself. Elizabeth and Sam are a dangerous pair."

Without another word, she got up and went into the house. I wondered what was going on and whether I was supposed to follow her inside.

A few minutes later, Myma returned, holding a small cloth bag tied with a coarse string. "Carry this with you at all times," she said, handing it to me. "Maybe it will help. It's stronger than garlic.

"Don't open it!" she cautioned, when she saw me trying to undo the string. I fingered the bag instead and could feel the shape of a root inside it.

Myma also held a small bottle. She opened it and sprinkled my head with a brown liquid that smelled like alcohol.

As she sprinkled, she mumbled something that I couldn't hear. "What are you saying?" I asked. "What is this?"

"It's just some words I learned from my mother," she said, "to protect you."

The day wasn't beautiful for me anymore. It was clear that Elizabeth had tricked us all and kept us in the dark about her devious motives.

I walked back home feeling discouraged and unsafe. As the heat warmed the alcohol that Myma had sprinkled on my head, I began smelling, I thought, like the bottom of a whiskey glass. The scent of the root she'd given me was a little better. I'd put it in my bra, where it gave off a mild, woodsy aroma.

Back at the house, there was no sign of Elizabeth's car. Just as I climbed the stairs and collapsed in exhaustion on the front porch, Caesar pulled into the driveway. I sighed and called Russell. I was depressed and hot and definitely didn't feel like socializing with Caesar or anyone else. But since I was already on the porch, I *had* to be sociable. I told myself I'd keep it short.

"H-h-hello Miss Finch," Caesar said politely, tipping his hat as he got out of his car. It was strange how his stutter came and went.

"Hello, Mr. Caesar," I said with a weak smile.

He took a seat on the porch and asked politely, "H-how is your research going?"

This was curious; he'd never shown much interest in our fieldwork before. "Well, um, we heard some stories about Brer Rabbit," I said.

He nodded courteously, but I could tell that Brer Rabbit wasn't what he was really interested in. "We also learned a song about Brer Fox," I offered.

He nodded again, and then asked bluntly, "What about Big Jack?"

"Didn't Sam tell you that we went to the little island with him to find Big Jack's cabin?" I asked a little sharply. "Didn't he tell you about what happened to Sierra?" I didn't want to think about that night.

"I-I haven't seen Sam lately," Caesar said with a shrug. Just like when I was talking to him before, I had a feeling he was lying.

I told him about rowing out to the old slave cabin and about the horrible way that Sierra had died.

He kept nodding as I spoke but didn't say anything in response. On the spur of the moment, I thought I'd try to test how much he knew. "We found the treasure, you know," I said in a calm voice, as though it was a very ordinary thing. "It was buried in a corner of the cabin."

He merely nodded again. *Wouldn't a normal person want to know what the treasure was?*

His reaction just heightened my suspicions. "Do you know anything about Big Jack's treasure, Caesar? Did you ever hear any stories about it?"

"I-I told you before that I don't know anything about Big Jack," he said hastily. Then he added in a husky whisper, as though he was betraying a secret, "P-p-people say be careful of Elizabeth and Sam."

Abruptly, he stood up and quickly descended the stairs. Walking faster than I'd ever seen him move before, he got in his car and backed out of the driveway, spinning his tires a little in the sand.

This was the second warning about Elizabeth and Sam—this time from someone who was supposed to be Sam's close friend. My head was pounding now, and I went inside and lay on the bed. Heat, alcohol, garlic, and the woodsy smell from the pouch wafted around me in a steamy cloud. I hoped the combination was strong enough to keep me safe until the happy day when I could leave St. Pierre.

When I awakened from my nap, it was dusk, and the house was as silent as it had been in the morning. I found Russell on the back porch again, eating a peanut butter and jelly sandwich. "Where's Elizabeth?" I asked him.

"The hell if I know. I guess she's still with Sam." I rolled my eyes.

"Hey, I overheard your conversation with Caesar," he added. "Why do you think he came by?"

"It was kind of strange. Almost like he was checking up on us. Can you believe that he hadn't heard any of the story from Sam?"

"No, that seemed strange to me too. And what was up with that thing he said about Elizabeth and Sam?"

I was just about to answer when we saw headlights reflecting off the outhouse and heard the sound of a car, followed by footsteps around the front of the house. "Russell, Finch, are you here?" Elizabeth called out. "The house is so dark."

"We're back here," I said coolly. She came onto the back porch, resetting her hair with her fingers. She looked a little rumpled but at first glance I didn't see any fresh bruises.

"Did you have a productive day at Sam's?" I asked sarcastically.

She looked at Russell, then me, and said primly, "Yes, I did." *Bitch, please*, I thought. *I'm on to you now.*

"Do you have the book?" Russell asked.

"Not yet; but maybe tomorrow."

With that, she went into her bedroom and closed the door on our questioning faces.

40

Elizabeth

June 16

Today, I told Russell and Finch I was going to Sam's place, but in fact I went back to the courthouse. The photograph that Sam claimed was taken when he was a child had only reinforced my questions about who he was and his relationship to St. Pierre. As it turned out, what I discovered at the courthouse was not at all what I expected. In fact, it was a turning point…and not a good one.

Things started off well enough. When I entered the tax office, one of the army of middle-aged white women who worked there greeted me. This one sported upswept salt-and-pepper hair and either newly trendy or vintage kitten glasses.

"Hello again. I remember you from the other day," she said cheerily. "I believe you're the teacher from Chicago? My name is Shirley Baker; let me know if you need any help."

I didn't waste energy correcting her about my job title and instead got down to work with a pile of tax records.

My pleasant mood soon turned to confusion.

As I already knew, multiple men named Samuel Dent were associated with the house in the graveyard. There was the Samuel Dent who'd purchased the house in 1910, signing the papers in elegant Copperplate script. For ten years, he'd paid his annual property taxes in person, but from 1920 onward they were paid by bank draft. The records did not show where those drafts originated.

Then, abruptly, another man named Samuel Dent resumed paying the taxes in person. This was ten years ago, when the Sam I knew moved to St. Pierre.

So had there been three Samuel Dents—Sam's grandfather, his father, and himself—or two? If his grandfather had bought the house at a young age and lived long enough, it was possible that just two generations were involved.

Fortunately, I was able to access census files through the courthouse's computers, and I turned to them next. At the very least, I would be able to find out who had lived in the Dent household in 1910 and 1920, and that might shed some light on the mystery.

The census showed that in 1910 a thirty-year-old man named Samuel Dent, his twenty-six-year-old wife, Caroline Southward Dent, and his six-year-old son, Samuel Dent Jr., lived on St. Pierre island.

This family could be the trio I'd seen in the photograph at Sam's house, except that he'd said *he* was the boy in the photograph. If that were true, he'd be an elderly man by now. Even if the photograph was more recent than it appeared to be, Sam would be much older than he was now if he was the little boy in it. Strange.

In the 1920 census, the three Dents, appropriately aged by ten years, still lived on St. Pierre. Subsequent censuses had no listings for the family.

Stumped where the twentieth century was concerned, I decided to go back in time. Were there Dents on St. Pierre *before* 1910? What about Samuel Dent's wife, Caroline? Fortunately, I had her maiden name and could use that to learn something about her family history.

Caroline's history was the first shock of the day. As best as I could tell from my analysis of a combination of census, death, military, and tax records, Caroline Southward Dent, born in 1884, was the out-of-wedlock, mixed-race daughter of a white man named William Southward. The 1860 census listed William Southward's age as twenty-two, his residence as St. Pierre, and his occupation as "plantation overseer." After serving in the Confederate army during the Civil War, Southward had apparently returned to St. Pierre, married, and purchased the property where Sam lived now. In his forties, he'd fathered several children by a Black woman named Hannah. Interestingly, Hannah had given the children William's last name, perhaps to force him to acknowledge their paternity.

The records showed that when Samuel Dent Sr. purchased the house by the graveyard in 1910, it was from William Southward, his wife's father. *William Southward, an overseer, was probably both the namesake and descendent of the man who'd killed Big Jack.* If so, then Sam was his descendant too. What a strange coincidence with our search for the book of secrets!

Or was it a coincidence? A hunch tied my stomach in knots and sent a chill down my spine. My legs felt funny too, perhaps from Sam's goddamned blows. I stood up and walked around to clear my head and get my circulation flowing. One of the clerks looked up questioningly, and I smiled to assure her that I was fine.

I sat down again and scoured various records from the 1860s, trying to locate the plantation where William Southward had been overseer. Many records had been lost during and after the Civil War, but eventually I was able to find what I was looking for.

It was a fortunate find—but also very disturbing, for it partially confirmed my hunch. Yes, the property where Sam lived was once part of the plantation where Big Jack had lived and died. The plantation owner, one James Butler, had parceled off his land after the war, including the section he had sold to William Southward.

My stomach tightened again. If Sam lived on the same land where Big Jack had lived, then why had we gone all over the island looking for the cabin? Wouldn't he have known that it was somewhere near his house? What was he up to?

All of this was an unpleasant reminder of the many ways in which Sam had been less than forthcoming. I resolved then and there to dig into his history. Only, where to begin?

I started with the obvious—entering Sam's name and approximate age into a search engine—and ended up hours later, with the courthouse again about to close for the day, confronted by a cold truth that I struggled to accept.

I had gradually broadened my search from just St. Pierre to the whole country, hoping to find Sam's date of birth, the place, and his parentage. Logically, he should have been the grandson or great-grandson of Samuel Dent Jr., who was six years old in the 1910 census. But, in fact, there was no record in any state of a Samuel Dent born after 1904. It was always possible that a person could be omitted from a single census, but *every single one*? In fact, Samuel Dent Jr. had disappeared from US records entirely until he appeared in St. Pierre ten years ago.

I went back to the local files from ten years earlier and this time saw something that literally stopped me in my tracks. On a record that requested birth date in addition to other information, Sam had written June 4, 1904. When I'd first seen it, I'd thought it was a typo. Now it took on a new and frightening meaning. 1904? *1904?* I stared at the number, dumbfounded. That would make Sam over one hundred years old.

Our conversation from days before replayed in my head. When I'd said that it couldn't possibly be him in the old photo, he'd responded, "It's a mystery, isn't it? But you like a mystery."

It was a mystery indeed. If Sam had really been born in 1904, where had he gone after leaving St. Pierre? Why did he return years later? And why did he look so young?

I didn't even know where to start to find the answers to those questions. But in the meantime, something that had started in me as a dark suspicion was growing into a certainty.

If Sam was the grandson, great-grandson—whatever—of the overseer William Southward, he had probably grown up hearing about Big Jack, and especially about Big Jack's book. His mother would have taught him the story and the song, even if she had described them to him as local superstitions. What if Sam had come to St. Pierre ten years ago specifically to search for the book of secrets? What if his apparently innocent interest in my research—and basically everything he had led me to believe up to now—was a lie? Did that explain his sneering comment yesterday that he'd *let* me think I discovered the song about Big Jack?

Now I was back to my original question. Who was Sam Dent?

Or what is he? a terrified little voice inside my head asked.

My legs began aching again—sitting for such long periods wasn't helping my bruises to heal. I stood up and rubbed my thighs briskly to get the circulation going. My muscles twitched, and I told myself it was just a reaction to being rubbed. It wasn't something more troubling...it wasn't the sensation of snakes twisting underneath your skin that Sierra had described. No, of course not.

As I drove home, I developed a plan. I wanted to talk to Sam again. I wanted to confront him about his lies, and I wanted the truth.

I was going to have to be careful. If my suspicions were right, Sam and I were playing a far more dangerous game than I'd ever imagined. I'd known we were misleading the students—okay, I'd had my reasons for that—but I'd never dreamed that I was being misled too. Just the thought of that made my blood boil. As I sped down the road, I promised myself, "Tomorrow, Sam. Tomorrow it all comes out."

41

Finch

June 17

Today was the beginning of the end—the end of one part of my life and the start of another. Today, what began just a few weeks ago as a kind of an adventure—and then turned the corner into terror and Sierra's death—turned yet another corner and became something I still can't name...I guess you could say it became my new life. But first there was horror and more terror in store.

Of course, we didn't know it at the time. The day started the way most of them had up to then, with the three of us going over our plans for the day. No one mentioned Sierra, but I reflected on how just a few days ago she would have been part of the planning too.

"Are you going back over to Sam's?" I asked Elizabeth, using as casual a tone as I could muster. Russell looked back and forth at the two of us, checking the level of tension.

"Yes," she said tightly. "Do you want to come too?"

"Yes," Russell replied for me. "I want to see what's in the book. Why is Sam holding on to it anyway? What's the big deal with it? It's just a book."

Elizabeth pressed her lips together and didn't answer. "We'll go over there this morning. I'll call and let him know we're coming."

We drove to his house, retracing the route of a few nights earlier when we'd gone to the graveyard. In daylight, it wasn't nearly as spooky, of course. In fact, the graveyard seemed almost peaceful as Russell and I followed Elizabeth down the well-worn path that led to Sam's house. Nothing moved except for a light, friendly breeze that stirred the trees.

Up close, Sam's house was not what I expected. Because he was kind of a sharp dresser, I thought his house would be nice too, but it wasn't.

In daylight, I saw that it was an ancient, spooky two-story building made of wood and tabby—oyster shells—like Big Jack's cabin. Large wooden shutters covered windows whose glass was cloudy with age. Just like our house, the shutters and wooden trimming were painted blue for protection from evil spirits. Thinking about what that blue meant always made me feel uneasy.

Like most of the houses on St. Pierre, Sam's was raised above ground level to protect it from floods and the high water table. Some houses were lifted on cinder blocks; his was on damp, mossy stones. The stones—and the house itself—looked as if nothing had changed in a hundred years. The yard, such as it was, was scruffy and untended and blended into the tufts and mounds of the surrounding graveyard. Creepy.

As we approached, I saw someone familiar descending the house's rickety wooden stairs. It was Myma! I had never seen her outside of her yard.

Her head was bound in a white cloth, and she was smoking her little pipe. In her hand she carried what looked like a bundle of plants.

"Hi, Miss Myma," I called as I walked down the path.

She looked at me and nodded but didn't speak. Then she looked back over her shoulder, and I saw Sam standing in the shadowy doorway, watching us. Something about him reminded me of a predator—a patient cheetah or hawk, waiting to catch its prey. He was dressed in dark clothes as usual, but for once he wasn't wearing a hat.

"Miss Myma, do you want a ride home?" I asked.

"No, Miss Finch," she answered briefly and trudged past me down the path through the graveyard and onto the road. Watching her, I wondered what she had been doing at Sam's.

When I turned back around, I saw Elizabeth and Russell going into the house, so I followed. Inside, it was dark—I could barely see after the bright morning sunshine—and musty.

The mustiness smelled familiar, like our own house, and with a jolt of recognition, I realized that both houses smelled like garlic. Garlic! More protection from spirits. My chest tightened momentarily, and I instinctively felt threatened.

"So you'd like to see the book," Sam said with a gleam in his eye and that predatory look again. "Why not? Let's take a look."

He waved toward some chairs and left the room. Like the house, the chairs were ancient, with stiff seats that felt like they were stuffed with straw or horsehair. From the walls of the room, glassy eyes stared down at us from faded photographs—just like Caesar's relatives at our house. More photographs were on the mantle. The suggestion that Sam was part of a larger family was jarring; he seemed so solitary.

There were strange things in the room too: in one corner, there was an egg with a small glass of brown liquid next to it, and in another corner, there was a sheaf of dried plants.

I caught Russell's eye and motioned toward the egg and glass with a "What's up with that?" expression on my face. He looked equally mystified.

When Sam reentered the room, he was carrying the cloth bundle we'd last seen in Big Jack's cabin. By then, my eyes had gotten accustomed to the dim light, and I saw that the cloth was an old quilt.

As Sam pulled a small wooden table into the center of the room and laid the bundle on it, Russell asked, "Why is there an egg in the corner with that glass next to it?"

"Oh, that's nothing," Sam said.

"Nothing?" Russell echoed.

"It's just something we do around here," Sam added by way of explanation. He looked around at us and said briskly, "Let's see what we have here."

I glanced over at Elizabeth, who seemed genuinely excited. Her cheeks were flushed, and her eyes were bright. Maybe the rough sex paid off after all, I thought to myself bitterly.

Sam began gently removing the quilt, which was rotted in places and spotted with mold and dirt from its long repose in Big Jack's cabin. He folded it and placed it carefully on one of the chairs. His slow, respectful motions impressed me.

Now the book of secrets lay on the table before us.

It was smaller than I expected, about six inches square, with a dark-brown leather cover. The leather was worn but intact and unmarked by any writing or designs. Sam slowly opened the cover, and I held my breath in anticipation, wondering what was coming next.

He turned to the book's first page. The thick beige paper was blank. He lifted another page, and then another. Page after thick beige page, it was the same thing. The pages were blank. The book of secrets was empty.

42

Finch
June 17

For a few moments, we all just stared at the table in shocked surprise. I looked questioningly at Elizabeth, whose brown face was actually ashen.

Suddenly, she jumped to her feet and pointed at Sam. "What is this?" she accused. "This isn't the book we found in Big Jack's cabin. This is nothing!"

Sam answered her smoothly, "What are you talking about? How do you know this isn't Big Jack's book? Maybe we let ourselves be fooled by an old story."

"Bullshit!" she shouted. "You switched the books. I know this isn't Big Jack's book. Big Jack's book is the book of secrets. Do you think I'm stupid? Do you think I went through everything"—she waved one arm dramatically—"for a blank leather book wrapped in a quilt?"

Elizabeth's reaction to Sam confirmed all my theories and growing suspicions. She had always known that the Big Jack song was about a book. She had lied all along about Big Jack's treasure.

A cold thrill went down my spine, and the ending of the song played in my head:

> Don't disturb Big Jack's secrets
> *Keep away; keep away*

Don't try to read his book
Shut your eyes; shut your eyes
It's the book of life and death
Stay away! Stay away!
And you'll be cursed just to look
Stay away! Stay away!

I remembered what Miss Massie had said: *"Big Jack's secrets are for him alone, but now it's too late."* And Miss Myma had said, *"Now Elizabeth has put you in danger."*

My anger boiled over. "You lied to us," I said, shouting to be heard over Elizabeth's argument with Sam. "You said the song was about treasure, when you knew it was about a book. Did you know it was cursed too? What have you gotten us into?"

"Oh, shut up," she shouted back, her face red now, her eyes blazing. "You stupid little girl, don't you know how important this book is?"

"Is it more important than Russell and me?" I hurled back. "Is it more important than Sierra?"

"Yes," she hissed, "it is."

Elizabeth turned back to Sam. They both stood, tense and poised like angry cats.

Russell sat, looking like a frightened child. I knew how he felt. I was furious, but I also felt powerless. Elizabeth had used us, and now we were trapped in the web she'd spun.

But where was the book? If this wasn't the book of secrets, where was it? Miss Massie said it was too late, which meant that the book was somewhere. Was Sam hiding it?

Suddenly, Elizabeth lunged across the table toward Sam. Now I was paralyzed, like Russell. I had never seen anything like this before.

She grabbed Sam's neck with both hands, as if to strangle him. They tussled violently. The table overturned, and the book fell on the floor. Russell and I jumped up, knocking our chairs over in the rush to get out of the way.

Sam wrestled Elizabeth to the floor and punched her face repeatedly. Meanwhile, she clawed him, drawing blood. Neither spoke; there was just the horrid sound of their grunting breath and struggling bodies, punctuated by the sickening percussion of Sam's fists.

"Stop," I screamed desperately. "Stop!"

I threw myself on top of Sam, while Russell pulled his arms, trying to intercept his slamming blows.

We struggled, panting and knocking over furniture, until we had successfully separated Sam and Elizabeth. She lay curled on the floor, choking and sobbing. Her nose was bleeding badly, and her mouth was cut. There was blood in her hair, on Sam's clothes, and mixed with the dust on the floor.

In the dim light of the darkened room, Sam's face looked oddly white for a moment, like the picture I'd seen of Baron Samedi.

He scrambled to his feet, adjusted his clothes—so vain!—and screamed at us, "Get out of here!" His face was dark with anger, twisted and ugly.

Russell and I pulled Elizabeth to her feet and dragged her to the door and down the steps. She was gasping for breath, and her face was swollen. The bruises on it had already begun to turn purple. She was dirty and bloody—a complete mess.

I felt sorry for her, but I also wondered why in the world she had attacked Sam. That was just stupid. But bringing us down here was stupid too. What a dumb bitch, I thought angrily. She's reckless, greedy, and thoughtless.

With Elizabeth slung between us, Russell and I negotiated the path through the graveyard and pushed her into the car. Russell got the keys from her purse and drove us home.

The cheerful afternoon light contrasted so bizarrely with our experience at Sam's house that the fight almost felt like a dream—until I looked at the back seat where Elizabeth was slumped, her misshapen and discolored face propped against the handle of the door.

At the house, Russell and I dragged and carried her up the stairs and into her bedroom. She fell onto her bed like a sack of potatoes, groaning in pain. I went to the refrigerator and got some ice that I wrapped in a cloth. When I came back in her bedroom, she was lying flat on her back, staring at the ceiling.

"Elizabeth?"

"What?" she croaked.

"Here's some ice that you can use on, um, your face."

"Thanks," she said expressionlessly.

As I turned to leave, she spoke again. "Finch? Thanks for saving me from *him*. Tell Russell too."

"Sure," I answered, feeling a twinge of sympathy. "Get some rest. I'll check on you in a little while."

43

June 17

I went into the living room and fell into a chair, trying to gather my thoughts. I was exhausted. Russell sat there too, looking like a wreck. Our clothes were filthy from the fight with Sam, and I realized that I'd gotten cut too. There were nasty red streaks on my arms that stung and looked like they could be infected. I forced myself out of the chair and went outside to the pump to rinse the cuts. The cool water felt good, and I hoped it would wash out all the dirt from the fight. I heard Elizabeth groaning in her room, but I was too tired to check on her.

"Russell," I shouted. "Elizabeth is saying something. Can you go to her room?"

I heard the floorboards creak, and then a panicked "Finch? Come quick!"

Still dripping water from my arms and hands, I ran up the back stairs, into the house, and across to Elizabeth's bedroom.

She lay stretched across the bed in the same position I'd seen her in earlier. But now she was shiny with sweat. Her short dark hair was damp, and her clothes were sticking to her. Her skin was grayish, and now there were purplish-black bruises on her chest and arms in addition to the ones on her face.

"What happened to her?" Russell asked me, as if I knew. "She looks terrible!"

"I-I don't know," I said. My mind raced wildly. There were no clinics or doctors on the island.

"Should we call an ambulance?" he asked. I made a face.

"Do you really think an ambulance from Charleston would bother coming out to St. Pierre?"

"Oh yeah, you're right."

"I'd better get Myma," I said. "Maybe she'll know what to do."

I raced down the road in Elizabeth's car to Myma's house, jumped out, and pounded on the front door. For once, she wasn't sitting outside in the yard. At first, there was no response, and my heart sank. Then I heard sounds inside, and the door cracked open.

Frantically, I told her about Elizabeth's fight with Sam. "She could be dying!" I said urgently. "You have to help us!"

At first, Myma just looked at me without responding, and I feared that meant her answer was no. But then she turned quietly and walked toward the back of her small house.

I followed her inside and was surprised by how dimly it was lit, like Sam's. I looked around as I waited but couldn't see much. Bunches of plants dried in the corners of the small front room, hanging by cords. I smelled garlic and also the woodsy root that she'd given me the day before.

When Myma returned to the front room, she was wearing a jacket and hat and carrying a large, bulging purse. "Let's go," she said simply.

It was dusk by the time we got back to the house. Russell pointed the way to Elizabeth's room, and Myma went there immediately.

I asked him how Elizabeth was. "She looks terrible," he said, shaking his head. "She's started moving around"—he imitated the motion of someone in pain—"and she says she feels like there's something under her skin."

I looked at him, eyes wide. "Just like Sierra said before she died."

Myma came out of the room. Her face sagged, and she looked defeated. "There is powerful hoodoo working on Elizabeth," she announced. "Was there blood spilled during the fight?"

We nodded. "Yes, there was blood on the floor and on both of them. I don't know if it was Sam's or Elizabeth's," I said. "I got scratched up too," I added, and glanced at the cuts on my arms. They seemed to be improving.

"Sam is using Elizabeth's blood against her," Myma announced firmly. "I am doing what I can, but he has powers that he can use against me."

She went back into Elizabeth's bedroom and closed the door behind her.

Russell and I choked down some dinner. We weren't very hungry. Maybe an hour later, there was a bloodcurdling scream from Elizabeth's bedroom, and we both rushed in.

Myma was standing at the foot of the bed. Her gray hair had come loose and wildly framed her mahogany face. Her eyes burned fiercely. She had ringed Elizabeth's bed with candles that she must have brought in her bag from home. In the flickering, golden light, we saw Elizabeth's twisted and writhing body.

Her eyes had rolled up in her head until just the whites showed. Her mouth was still open in the aftermath of the terrible scream we'd heard. With bottomless horror, I watched as a greenish snake pushed its head from between her lips and licked its forked tongue in the air. Meanwhile, huge, snakelike shapes moved restlessly beneath the skin of Elizabeth's arms and legs, as though they too were trying to escape her body. She moaned, cried, and shrieked unconsciously as the monstrous shapes twisted ceaselessly within her.

44

The air was thick with the scent of the burning candles, Elizabeth's sweating body, and something herbal that must have been burning too. I looked at Myma, terrified. She was our only hope.

Her face stern and determined, she extracted a small bottle from her purse and sprinkled the liquid from it on Elizabeth's body. "Leave her, I say!" Myma commanded firmly. Then she said some words I didn't understand, in another language. "Leave her!" she repeated.

Nothing happened to the snakes; they continued to move horribly beneath Elizabeth's skin. Their motion reminded me of the loathsome vines that had reached out of the ground to snare us in the graveyard by Sam's house.

I jumped backward as a gleaming green head suddenly broke through the skin on the palm of one of Elizabeth's hands. Elizabeth's arm lifted, and for a moment I thought she was coming back to life, but the skin hung slackly—it was only the force of the snake's movement at work. It coiled its hideous gleaming body and hissed at Myma, but Myma didn't flinch. She was not afraid.

In the thick, smoky air, filmy shapes and faces began appearing before me. They obscured my vision, and it was like being in a thick fog. I thought I saw Sierra—was that possible?—and Caesar as well, just for a moment. Sam's face hung in the air too, smiling maliciously. I struck out angrily, trying to get the apparitions to dissipate. "You're not here!" I shouted. "Go away!" They wafted away momentarily, just as the faces had done in the graveyard, then regrouped and surrounded me. I felt like I was going crazy.

Myma motioned for me to be quiet. With difficulty, I controlled myself. I looked over in Russell's direction and saw that mists surrounded him too. He twisted like a dervish, swatting and swearing under his breath. Once, he shouted, "Fuck off!" and Myma quickly silenced him.

Meanwhile, she continued talking in the strange foreign language. She walked around Elizabeth's bed, sprinkling her with the contents of bottles she pulled from her purse. More and more snakes appeared as she walked, maliciously turning their heads toward her as though to mock her efforts to save Elizabeth. Their red tongues flicked in and out, and their yellow eyes glowed hatefully.

Abruptly, Myma fell to her knees by the side of the bed. The snakes surged toward her but then recoiled, repelled by a protective force that I couldn't see. Myma began singing. At first, I thought it was a church hymn, but then I recognized a more ancient melody and realized it must have been an African song.

Myma got back on her feet and gradually circled Elizabeth's bed, still singing. The minor tones reminded me of the song I'd heard in Big Jack's cabin. She shuffled her feet in a kind of dance and moved her hands repeatedly toward the snakes in an outward motion, as though she was pushing them away. At first they were unresponsive; in fact, they surged angrily toward her. If the snakes' bodies hadn't been tethered to Elizabeth, Myma might have been physically attacked, but she stayed out of their reach.

Patiently, she circled the bed, again and again, and gradually the snakes fell back, hissing and writhing as though they were in pain. Eventually they lay limply on Elizabeth's body, covering her with their terrible green shapes. Elizabeth was silent. I thought she was breathing, but I wasn't sure. The room was hot and still smoky from the candles, but the spirits and faces that had tormented Russell and me had vanished.

Myrna collapsed into a chair, clearly worn out. Staring at Elizabeth's unmoving body, she said, "I will stay here with Elizabeth. I used all of my power, but I don't know if it was enough. Only time will tell."

"Get some sleep," she ordered Russell and me. "Come back in the morning."

Later, just as I was finally falling asleep, my head swirling with images from the scene in Elizabeth's bedroom, I heard a creak, and my bedroom door opened. Startled, I sat up straight, ready to run, until with relief I recognized Russell's silhouette. He quietly stepped inside my bedroom, and, equally silently, I lifted the cover so that he could climb into the bed. We held each other wordlessly for a long time, and I appreciated how his warm bulk made me feel more secure than I had in a long time. Eventually, we both fell asleep like a couple of old married people.

Sometime during the night, I woke up to the soft sensation of Russell's gentle but persistent kisses. "Finch," he said tenderly. "You know I've wanted to do this for a long time. I just didn't know how you would react."

Without really thinking about it, I moved closer and felt his erection pressing against me. I opened my thighs and wrapped my legs around him.

The sex that followed was a fantastic release after all the horrible events of the day. I felt a little guilty about doing it in the same house where Elizabeth was in agony, but I also felt like I deserved a break. And it felt good. Afterward, we fell back asleep, slippery with sweat and satisfied.

45

Finch
June 18

In the morning, Russell and I woke up in each other's arms. He prodded my leg with his morning erection, but I pushed him away with a smile.

"We have to check on Elizabeth," I whispered. I opened my door slowly and looked around the living room, feeling a little guilty that somebody—who? Myma?—might see me getting out of bed with Russell.

To my relief, the coast was clear. The early-morning sky was grayish, and I heard a few birds cheeping. There was no sign of Myma.

Timidly, Russell and I opened Elizabeth's bedroom door, dreading what we might see.

She lay on the bed, still covered by the inert bodies of the snakes. Her sweat-soaked clothes gave off a sour smell. Her eyes were closed, and her arms and legs were twisted in painful positions.

Myma was asleep in the chair where we'd left her, her head lowered toward her chest and her loose gray hair gently bobbing in time with her breathing. I inched closer to Elizabeth and grasped her wrist to feel her pulse. One of the snakes suddenly reared up, and I screamed and jumped back, tripping on one of the candles and losing my balance. Just as suddenly, the snake fell back and was limp.

Awakened by my scream, Myma stirred to life and came over to the bedside. Unafraid of the snakes, she felt Elizabeth's chest and held her wrist. She held her cheek to Elizabeth's mouth to see if she was breathing. Finally, with a deep sigh she said, "She is gone."

It was devastating news. I suppose I shouldn't have been surprised, considering everything that had happened the night before, but still I'd hoped that Myma could somehow save Elizabeth.

I felt guilty all over again about having been with Russell when Elizabeth was dying. But still, what could I have done to help her? And Myma had told us to come back in the morning.

My thoughts swirled confusedly, and I slumped onto one of the dusty chairs in the front room. Russell collapsed into another one. He looked as defeated as I felt.

46

Finch

June 18

I don't know how long we sat there, not speaking, just staring into space. My head was beginning to hurt badly, and I was starting to feel strange sensations in my arms and legs. My muscles jumped from time to time, and I had the chills.

I hunched down in the chair and shivered. "Is it cold in here?" I asked Russell.

"Are you kidding?" he answered. "I'm burning up." Sweat was pouring down the sides of his face, and his shirt was damp. There wasn't a doctor for miles. If we were getting sick, we would be in trouble.

Elizabeth's bedroom door opened, and Myma came out, her back bent and her hair awry. Her feet shuffled as she walked, and her face was haggard with exhaustion. She looked at us with worried eyes. "Sam killed Elizabeth with powerful hoodoo, and it's going to get stronger. Now that he has the book of secrets, he has the power to harm many people."

"What book?" I asked, surprised. "At Sam's house last night, the book he showed us was blank. It was just an old cover and empty pages. That's why he and Elizabeth started fighting."

It was all less than a day ago, but so much had happened in the meantime that it felt like a million years had passed. I squeezed my temples as I mentally replayed the events; my headache was getting worse.

"Tell me exactly what happened after I left Sam's house," Myma said grimly, sitting down in one of the empty chairs. It creaked softly under her weight and released a few puffs of tired dust.

Russell and I described how Sam Dent had carefully unwrapped the book and Elizabeth's reaction when she found out there was nothing in it...no poems, no songs, no words or even drawings—nothing; therefore, no secrets. We told how we had dragged Elizabeth out of Sam's house and brought her back to our cottage before calling Myma for help.

Myma pursed her lips and touched the amulet around her neck. "You know that Elizabeth was right, don't you? That wasn't the real book."

"What?" Russell and I asked simultaneously. "How do you know?"

"Tell me again how Sam showed you the book," she answered cryptically.

It seemed like a minor detail, but Russell repeated how Sam had brought the book out, wrapped in an old piece of cloth.

"And was it a woven cloth, like *kente*?"

"No, it wasn't woven; it looked more like a quilt," he said, after some thought.

"You see, there it is!" Myma announced, nodding her head for emphasis. "The real book is wrapped in a very old woven cloth, a cloth that Big Jack brought with him from his homeland. If the book you saw was in a quilt, that proves that Sam showed you the wrong one."

An image came into my throbbing head: on the night when we'd gone to Big Jack's cabin, the night of Sierra's horrible death, the bundle that Sam dug up was wrapped in a woven cloth that reminded me of pieces I'd seen in a textile museum. The cloth I'd seen at Sam's house yesterday was old and tattered, but it was definitely a pieced quilt. I'd been so caught up in the drama of finally seeing the book of secrets that I hadn't even noticed the difference at the time.

"B-but where is the real book then?" I sputtered.

"Sam has it," Myma said firmly. "He has it, and you have to get it from him before it's too late."

She turned and looked me hard. I shivered from her fierce glance and from the chills that had started up again.

"You have to get it from him," she repeated. "He probably hid it in Big Jack's cabin. You have to go back there and find it and destroy it."

"Destroy the book of secrets?"

"Yes, it is too powerful; that's why Big Jack died to protect it. That was his way of keeping it from falling into the wrong hands."

47

Finch

June 18

My heart sank. "Miss Myma, I feel horrible. My head is killing me and my arms and legs feel funny. I don't know if I can go back to Big Jack's cabin. We'll have to cross that graveyard again, and what if—" Overwhelmed at the very thought of repeating that nightmare journey, I broke off.

"I'm getting sick too," Russell chimed in, "except I feel hot, and Finch feels cold. Something is wrong with us."

"That is Sam's hoodoo," Myma said. "He is working you right now with his roots and spells."

"How?" I asked.

"Did you bleed in the fight yesterday? Did he draw blood?"

My stomach turned as I remembered the dusty scratches on my arms. Without answering Myma, I rolled up my sleeve and looked at them. A few hours ago, the scratches had looked like they were healing. Now they were raised and red, as though they were infected.

"Did you lose blood or hair?" Myma asked Russell.

"I must have," he answered. "I was in the fight too, and now I feel like shit." His face was shiny with perspiration.

"We don't have much time," she said briskly. "Sam is attacking you, and his magic is strong. You have to get the book from him. We'll go to my home first, and I'll do what I can to protect you. "

I didn't like the sound of "I'll do what I can," but we didn't have many alternatives.

"Can you make my headache go away?" I pleaded. "I can't go back to Big Jack's cabin the way I feel now; I'm too weak."

"Yes, I can make you and Russell feel better for now…but we don't have much time. You have to get started."

We locked up the house, and Russell drove the three of us to Myma's. He twitched from time to time as though he was in pain, but I think he was in better shape than I was.

I rested my head on the back of the seat and closed my eyes. I felt like I was sinking underground, surrounded by snakes, pain, and crawling things. My head hurt so much that I could barely think or move. I knew we should report Elizabeth's death, but that would mean being asked a lot of questions, and how would I answer them? Who would believe me if I said a snake came out of her mouth and there were spirits in the air?

I answered my own question: no one would believe our story. They would arrest us under suspicion of murder, and we might never get free. No, it was impossible to deal with Elizabeth's death right now, and we weren't going to; we were going back to Big Jack's cabin.

We carefully wrapped Elizabeth's limp body in a sheet and put her in the trunk of the car. Myma said she would figure out what to do about her. I was just grateful that I didn't have to.

Inside Myma's house, it was stuffy and hot, but peaceful, and aromatic from her collection of roots and herbs. It felt like a safe place to be. She went into her mysterious back room and returned shortly with two glasses of an unappetizing-looking brown liquid that she instructed us to drink for our pains, chills, and fever. I literally held my nose—and still almost choked on the strong, bitter flavor. But the treatment worked, and half an hour later, I felt like myself again.

"That will help you for a while," Myma said. "As soon as you get the book from Sam Dent, you will begin to feel better without my medicine." *As soon as...*I liked her optimism.

Myma disappeared in the back of her house again, and I think we dozed for a while in her front room. I woke up feeling more energetic than I had in the morning. I wasn't looking forward to what Russell and I had to do, but I was ready to get started.

She came back in the room with plates of rice and cold fried fish. "You must eat something," she commanded. "You'll need the energy." While we ate, she left the room again and then returned with her hands full.

"These will help you find Sam and fight him," she said, placing a bottle, a little bag, and some candles on a table.

"If you know what to do, why can't you come with us?" I asked. "Why are we going by ourselves?"

"You are already under Sam's control," Myma answered ominously. "From the time when he first marked you with the necklaces, he has been exerting his power against you. That is why you have to fight him now. You have to free yourselves from his control."

My hand went to my neck. "The necklaces! But Sam said they were for our protection!"

"Well, they did protect you," she said, "when he wanted them to. But you were always under his control."

With a rising feeling of doom, I said, "The first time we went to Big Jack's cabin, we had to cross a graveyard. Crazy stuff happened... there were vines that came alive and tried to pull us down into the earth, and horrible faces that surrounded us. I thought the necklaces kept it from being worse."

"Yes," Myma said patiently, "the necklaces kept you safe from Sam's army; he wanted it to be that way."

"Sam's army?" Russell repeated questioningly.

Myma gave a dry laugh. "That's what we call them. He controls roaches, vines, spirits—oh, many things. He uses them to get his way in the world. And now he has the book that he has wanted for such a long time."

She looked at us directly, unsmiling. "He needed help to get the book. He needed blood, and he chose Sierra's. He needed her death to release the book from Big Jack's protection. Elizabeth went along with it, because she wanted the book too. And she didn't care about the three of you; she would do whatever it took to get what she wanted."

At this news, I felt like the earth was crumbling beneath my feet. I was falling, falling, falling, and soon would be swallowed up. My ears rang, my heart pounded, and my chest was tight. Yes, I'd stopped liking and trusting Elizabeth a long time ago, but this? She had betrayed Sierra to get her hands on a book?

"The first time I saw you with Elizabeth, I felt sorry for you," Myma said. "I didn't say anything, but I had a feeling that she'd lied to you. I had a feeling she was using you, and now I know I was right. She put the three of you in danger, and now you have to save yourselves. And you have to save us too," she added. "The power from the book will hurt us all."

"What can Sam do with it?" I asked. "What are you afraid of?"

"It's the book of life and death," she said, repeating the words of the song. "He can use it to control the living and the dead, and the living-to-be who haven't been conceived yet. He can reach into the hearts of men and make them do his bidding. He can command the winds and the rains. It is powerful magic that Big Jack brought from Africa, and it was never meant to fall into the hands of people like Sam who haven't been prepared to use it wisely.

"Sam isn't what you think he is," she added darkly. "He'll fight you for the book, and then you'll see his true colors."

"Do you mean that he'll try to kill us?"

"Well yes, he'll try to do that," she said matter-of-factly. "That's why I have to protect you. But there's more…" She trailed off.

"What?" I asked, squeezing her hand nervously. "Tell me!"

"He's very old, you know."

"He is?" Russell asked in surprise.

"Yes, he's very old, and for years he has been studying the ancient African arts."

I didn't know what Myma meant by "ancient African arts," but it made me shiver with fear and anticipation.

Before I could ask about it, she changed the subject. Looking out the window at the sun, she said, "You need to go while the tide is still out."

She turned toward us and motioned to her throat. "Take off those necklaces from Sam. I have better protection for you."

I pulled on the cord of the garlic necklace Sam had given me. As it broke, I felt a sharp, painful twinge deep inside, just for a moment. Russell winced too.

"Did you feel something just then?" I asked him.

"Yeah." He made a face. "You know how people talk about feeling like someone walked over their grave? I felt something weird like that."

Myma asked if I still had the root she'd given me before, and I pulled the little warm bag from my bra and showed it to her.

"Good, keep it with you at all times." She handed me something that felt like matted hair and said, "Add this to the root."

She gave Russell a little bag like mine and gestured that he should put it in his pocket.

"What is this stuff?" I asked. "It looks like somebody's hair."

"It *is* hair," she answered. "Sam's hair. Do you remember seeing me at his house yesterday? That's when I got it, when he wasn't looking. It has power against him. Use it if you need to." I shivered again.

"These candles will light your way if you find yourselves in dark places," she continued, holding up dark-yellow candles that were etched with strange markings.

She handed two candles to each of us one along with boxes of matches. The candles were heavy and felt oily.

"What do these markings mean?" I asked.

"Keep the candles and matches dry," Myma said, evading my question.

With a sigh—knowing that was all she was going to say—I put my candles in the messenger bag I normally used for my notebooks and laptop, and Russell pushed his into his pockets.

Finally, Myma handed me a small bottle with a cork and said, "Don't be afraid to ask Big Jack for help; he will hear you."

"Big Jack is alive?" I asked in astonishment. I was confused now; deeply confused.

"No, Big Jack is in the land of spirits, but this liquid"—she gestured toward it—"will help him hear you."

"What is it?" I asked.

"It's ancient power," she answered mysteriously. "People fear toads, but there is power they can give us."

I had no idea what that was supposed to mean. "What do I do with it?" The liquid had a milky, bland appearance; it certainly didn't look powerful.

"You'll know when the time comes," she answered cryptically.

"What about me?" Russell demanded. "Do I get one of those bottles too?"

Myma looked at him and said simply, "Finch is the one who needs it." She looked out at the sun again and said, "Time is passing. You have to go."

"One other thing," she added, as we walked to the car. "Beware of Caesar Cummings; he is one of Sam's army."

48

June 18

As we drove to Sam Dent's house—and the graveyard we'd have to cross to get back to Big Jack's cabin—I thought about how, in less than a week, we'd lost both Sierra and Elizabeth to horrible deaths because of Sam and the book of secrets. Now we were headed for a showdown with him. Armed with what? Candles, necklaces, roots, and a bottle of what could be milk for all I knew? My stomach churned, and a dull throb in my head reminded me of the blinding pain I'd felt earlier in the day. We didn't have much time. How was this story going to end? Could it possibly end well?

I kept my misgivings to myself as we drove down the narrow, sandy roads leading to Sam's house. Night was falling, and shadows were gathering beneath the trees. The moon was in its waning stage now and hadn't risen yet. By the time we arrived at the graveyard, it was completely dark.

Fortunately, Elizabeth's flashlights were still in the back seat of the car. We each took one as Russell muttered grimly, "Let's do this."

"Do you think we'll find a canoe?" I asked anxiously.

"We'll find out, won't we?" he replied. Increasingly, our expedition felt to me like a fool's errand. But there was no turning back now.

It was a still, windless night, but as soon as we walked into the graveyard, I heard rustling sounds. The long fingers of moss hanging from the oaks seemed to sway and move menacingly.

Russell noticed it too. "Let's walk faster," he said in a low voice.

It was intensely dark, and the beams from our flashlights were pinpricks that just barely illuminated our path. I tripped on something and pointed my flashlight downward. The cool white of one of the gravestones reflected back into my eyes. Just a gravestone... maybe this wouldn't be so bad.

We walked on, quickly and quietly. I tripped again and looked down, hoping it was another gravestone. But this time it was very different. The ground was moving beneath my feet, just as it had when we'd come to the graveyard on Sunday night!

Suddenly a vine sprang to life and grabbed my ankle. It was a repeat of our earlier experience, but now we didn't have Sam's protective necklaces.

Abruptly, there were vines everywhere, muscling above the ground like green and brown arms. I felt them pulling at my feet, pulling me down into their demon world.

"Run!" Russell shouted.

I tried to, but as though in a dream, I could barely control my feet. I pulled as hard as I could; it felt like I was moving in slow motion. Nearby, Russell grunted and puffed. He jerked his feet, trying to free them from the vines.

From somewhere, the idea came to me that the flashlights might help us. With shaking hands, I trained mine on a vine that was spiraling up my leg. I heard something that sounded like a muted scream, and suddenly the vine fell backward.

"Use your flashlight!" I shouted at Russell. He did, and after some struggling, we were both able to pull free.

We picked up speed and began running toward the creek. As we passed under the hulking trees, the dangling moss writhed as though trying to grab our throats, and we had to use our arms to push it away.

A thick strand of moss wrapped itself around Russell's throat, and I clawed it off him with my hands. Again, I thought I heard tiny screams as I ripped the moss away, as though it were alive.

We gradually made our way toward the shore of the salt creek. It was slow going, and our struggles with the haunted vegetation were exhausting. Nonetheless, I was grateful that so far we'd been spared the ghostly voices and other visitations of Sunday night. In the back of my mind, I wondered when—and where—we would face off with Sam.

Finally, I smelled a familiar musky, damp smell and knew we were near the creek. The moon was just rising. In its pale light, I was surprised to see a silhouetted figure standing on the shore. Its back was turned to us, and it was partly in shadow.

I grabbed Russell's arm and pointed. We both stopped running and started walking toward the stranger. The person definitely wasn't Sam; it looked more like a woman. Who could it be?

She turned, and we saw it was Sierra. Sierra! Her face was expressionless and masklike, and her skin was dull and dry like brown clay.

"Sierra?" I said walking toward her. "Is that you?" It was a stupid question, because I knew she was dead, but I still felt compelled to ask. I remembered seeing her face for a moment when Elizabeth was dying. Was it possible that she *wasn't* dead?

Sierra looked at us blankly and then began coming toward us. I looked down and, to my horror, saw that she had no feet. "She's a ghost," I screamed, as I started running toward the creek. Russell followed, with Sierra gliding closely behind him.

Looking back over my shoulder, I saw her face shifting into terrifying shapes. Twisting as though made of soft, brown clay, it writhed and changed, becoming less and less human. Eventually, snakes shoved from her eyes and mouth and licked their vile tongues in our direction.

We ran away desperately, pushing our way through the brush at the side of the creek and avoiding the mud that we knew could trap our feet. As we ran, waves of mist rose from the banks of the creek.

Gradually, they took shape around us until once again we confronted the howling, gruesome faces of the slaves who'd never been buried properly.

Their tortured eyes and grimaced expressions surrounded us in every direction, while the din of their voices made it impossible to think. These desperate souls were part of Sam's army! Instead of giving them a proper burial, he used them for his evil purposes, just the way they had been used against their will when they were alive.

The spirits came up on every side and surrounded us so that we couldn't run. Russell and I huddled together on the shore, our ears filled with their sobs and cries. I could hear Sierra's voice too, moaning repeatedly, "Turn back. Finch, Russell, turn back. Stay away. Stay away."

49

Finch
June 18

Desperately, I reached into my bra and removed the bundle that Myma had given me. It was warm and aromatic. Just holding it reminded me of her and made me feel safer.

I gripped it tightly and thought, "If you have power against Sam, we need that power now!" Then I motioned to Russell to take his own bundle out.

Together, we held them up in front of us. At first, nothing happened. The mists seemed to grow thicker, and the voices got louder. My ears reverberated with the din. My confidence collapsed and was replaced by a sense of doom.

Suddenly, a strong wind blew across the water and pushed the mists and spirit faces away, clearing a path before us. The spirits' voices turned to low moans as they were forced to retreat. Sierra's distorted face withdrew as well. As it did, the snake protruding from her mouth hissed savagely, and its eyes gleamed malevolently.

Encouraged by this turn of events, we held our bundles higher in the air and slowly made our way toward the dock, keeping the spirits and Sierra at bay.

We found two canoes tied at the dock and the third one missing. Did that mean that Sam was already at Big Jack's cabin? We'd know the answer to that question soon enough.

The three-quarter moon peeked out from clouds that were beginning to gather on the horizon and lit the way to our island destination. Sierra, or what remained of her, stayed on shore, along with the slave spirits. I prayed they wouldn't follow us to Big Jack's island, the way they had before.

It was a quiet night, the only sounds being an occasional splash from the direction of the water or the lonely cry of a water bird. After our experiences getting this far, it seemed almost peaceful.

Russell and I were quiet too. We paddled steadily and without talking, as we gathered strength for the unknown struggle that lay ahead of us.

Eventually, the canoe nosed into the muddy shore of the island, and we jumped overboard to walk ashore. There was another canoe docked already, confirming that Sam—or someone—had arrived on the island before us.

The mud pulled at my shoes and made eerie sucking sounds as I walked. Was I hearing voices again, this time coming from the ground? I hoped not. I hoped it was just my tired mind playing tricks on me.

I dug in my pocket for some aspirin and ate them to ward off my returning headache. My arms and legs ached too—from Sam's magic or from running—and I wondered how long I could go on. I leaned over for a minute to gather myself, then looked over at Russell and whispered, "Showtime," as I straightened. His face was anxious, and I knew it mirrored my own.

Not knowing where else to go, we headed for the remains of Big Jack's cabin, plodding through the mud and following a little path through the tangled underbrush. Our previous trip down this path was a terrible memory that I tried to push from my mind. I couldn't let myself get distracted.

As we approached the pile of broken boards and shells that had once been Big Jack's cabin, I thought I heard faint sounds that could be voices and movement. I stopped in my tracks, and Russell motioned for me to hide behind some nearby bushes.

Moments later, as my eyes adjusted to the moonlight, I saw Sam standing in the rubble of Big Jack's cabin, moving boards around with a shovel. He was wearing a dark outfit as usual and was hatless. He lifted board after board and was clearly searching for something buried beneath them.

At one point, he put down his shovel and looked around. With a sinking sensation, I thought he had seen or heard us, but instead he commanded sharply, "Caesar, come over here."

Caesar emerged from under the shadowy trees, carrying a bulky armload of tools that he dropped near Sam. Eerily, he looked the same as the last time I'd seen him, wearing his familiar hat and walking stiffly.

"What do you want me to do?" he asked Sam, without the slightest stammer. Sam answered by lifting a board with his shovel. For the next few minutes, they cleared the rubble of the collapsed cabin together. They concentrated on the corner where Sam had first pulled the book of secrets—or what he told us was the book of secrets—from the ground.

We watched as Sam and Caesar cleared the boards away, pausing occasionally to wipe their faces, but never stopping. Then Sam commanded Caesar, "Stop!" and we saw him crouch near the ground. From that position, Sam dug with a trowel until he uncovered something that he lifted up.

It was a bundle wrapped in woven cloth. It looked like the bundle we'd seen on our first trip to Big Jack's island, not like the quilt-wrapped bundle he'd shown us at his house.

Sam laughed softly and said, "I fooled them, Caesar! I buried the book again before we left the island."

Caesar laughed too. "You very smart, Mas' Sam. You fooled them all."

"Of course Elizabeth figured out that I was lying," Sam said, "but by then I'd gotten what I needed from her. Stupid bitch!" His foolish sidekick Caesar laughed again in agreement.

"It's too bad we had to sacrifice Sierra; she was a cute kid," Sam continued. "But you have to do what you have to do."

"You have to do what you have to do," Caesar echoed stupidly.

I was furious that they could be so cavalier about other people's lives. "God damn you," I shouted, stumbling out from behind the bush where I'd been hiding.

Russell tried to pull me back, but I brushed him off. "God damn you both! You sacrificed Sierra for this stupid book, and you killed Elizabeth too."

"I had a feeling we weren't alone," Sam said to Caesar, ignoring me. "I could smell them and their little roots from Myma."

"*That* bitch betrayed me," he added, twisting his face. "We'll deal with her later."

I took a step forward. "Give me the book," I commanded Sam. "You don't deserve to have it."

He laughed and looked directly at me for the first time. "You want the book? Who are you? You don't even know its power or how to use it. Caesar, get rid of them!"

Caesar lunged toward us with the dirt-crusted shovel he was still holding, swinging it viciously from side to side. I screamed and hurriedly jumped aside, while Russell ran in the opposite direction.

Caesar couldn't pursue both of us at the same time, and I thought that gave us the upper hand. I had forgotten about the old boards from Big Jack's cabin though. In my haste to escape the slicing shovel blade, I tripped and fell.

Suddenly, Caesar was above me, swinging the shovel at my head. Sweat covered his dark-brown face, and his face was contorted with rage; I barely recognized him.

I screamed again and rolled across the old boards, wincing as nails and splinters tore at my skin. Seconds later, Caesar's shovel struck the ground where I'd just been lying, making a dull ringing sound as the metal rebounded from the packed earth.

As I struggled to my feet, I saw that Russell was standing behind Caesar with a board in his hands. He swung it hard and hit the side of Caesar's head. Caesar staggered, turned toward him, and then fell onto a pile of boards.

I scrambled up, grabbed a small board, and clobbered him again, hoping that the board wasn't too rotten to be effective. I wasn't violent by nature, but this felt like a life-or-death fight, and I'd seen what Caesar and Sam could do.

Caesar lay collapsed at my feet, his body curled as though he were asleep. I didn't know if I'd killed him or not, but I was relieved that at least he was out of commission.

Just then, there was a movement in the shadows, and Sam emerged holding the trowel he'd used to dig up the bundle. With a strong downward thrust, he dug the trowel into Russell's neck.

All my insides went cold as blood spurted and Russell sank to the ground like a stone. I ran to him and fell to my knees. Holding the wound on his neck, I helplessly watched his blood flow through my desperate fingers, as I cried and prayed that somehow I could save him.

50

June 18

I don't know how long I stayed like that, but Russell's body was cold when I straightened up and looked around. I was sitting in a pool of bloody mud, my body stiff and sore. The shock of Russell's death was like a weight in my chest.

In the moonlit gloominess of the ruined cabin, there was no sign of either Sam or Caesar. I felt cold fury toward them—icy, murderous rage. They had killed every member of the team, and I was determined to destroy them before they got me next.

Carefully resting Russell's body on some boards, I left the cabin and ran to where we'd left the canoe. Ours was still there, along with Sam's. Where could he and Caesar be? The wind was rising, and I heard the first rumbling of distant thunder.

I ran back toward the cabin, feeling my headache and body aches returning. Reaching in my pocket for more aspirin, I clumsily dropped the last two. The bottle Myma had given me fell too and rolled into the shadows under some bushes. Damn! I dug around frantically in the leaves and mud until I found it. But the aspirin were gone for good. Thunder rumbled again, louder this time.

I went back to where Sam and Caesar had cleared the ground searching for the book and scanned the ground with my flashlight, looking for something—I didn't really know what.

To my surprise, I saw a large hole near the smaller one where the book had been buried. I poked it with one of the broken boards and couldn't feel the bottom. I leaned down over it and thought I heard faint sounds. I also felt fresh air on my cheek. Dimly, I heard Sam shout, "Caesar!" Then the next words were muffled.

Could the hole be a tunnel of some kind? It was just large enough to accommodate a person's body. I wondered if it was something the slaves had built; maybe it was part of the Underground Railroad. Perhaps they had found solid ground amid the mud of the salt creeks.

I considered for a moment and decided that I had nothing to lose at this point. I had already lost everyone who mattered to me on St. Pierre. Guided by the frail beam of my flashlight, I lowered myself into the pitch-dark tunnel.

51

Finch

June 18

The air in the tunnel was warm and close, but fresher than I expected because of the slight breeze that occasionally brushed my cheeks. The tunnel's floor was gravelly but even. The ceiling was low, forcing me to walk hunched over. I couldn't move quickly. As I descended, I heard thunder reverberating above me.

I groped along by the light of the flashlight, constantly turning my head back and forth, looking for movement and listening for sounds. Whenever my head grazed the top of the tunnel, loose rocks and bits of shell broke free, and I worried about the whole thing collapsing and burying me forever. Even Myma wouldn't know where to find me.

I wondered where the tunnel led and listened for sounds of Sam and Caesar. Above me, the thunder was rumbling continuously, only slightly muted by the thick walls of earth. Without aspirin to dull the pain, I was beginning to feel weak. I didn't know how much longer I could continue.

Deeper I went. Now Sam's and Caesar's voices were louder, as though the distance between us was shrinking. At the same time, a dim glow from the flashlight or candle they were using to navigate the inky darkness also became faintly visible. I slowed my pace and crept along. The rocky tunnel walls closed in closer and closer around me, forcing me to descend. If I wanted to turn around, it would be impossible.

I descended more, feeling the scrape of the narrowing walls on my arms and legs. It was like entering a tomb. My heart beat rapidly and unevenly.

To my relief, the tunnel abruptly widened into a large cave. I stopped near the entrance and dropped down behind some sheltering rocks to gather myself. Inside, the cave was bright with warm golden light that was a sudden and welcome contrast to the darkness of the tunnel. Peering from my vantage point, I saw that flickering candles ringed the floor and illuminated the walls almost to the distant ceiling. Sam and Caesar were standing in the center of the fiery circle. In the shimmering light, I saw that the walls that surrounded them were densely covered in painted symbols. The symbols rose out of sight and seemed to dance before my tired eyes.

The cave must have been a sacred space of some kind, built by the slaves and hidden from their masters by the tunnel that people could use to come and go without detection. The symbols resembled the ones carved into the candles that Myma had given Russell and me. Russell—I suppressed the painful memories that his name evoked and concentrated on the scene in front of me.

Sam was shouting again at Caesar, who knelt like a beaten dog before him. "Obey my bidding!"

"Yes, Mas'," Caesar complied, looking down at the hard mud floor of the cave.

Sam's back was toward me. I saw the woven cloth with the book of secrets lying at his feet. The book was open, and it looked as though Sam was about to use it in some kind of ceremony.

My painful legs forced me to shift my weight to get comfortable, and in the process I accidentally dislodged some rocks. They pattered softly onto the floor of the cave. At the movement, Sam turned, and I caught my breath in surprise.

He was grotesquely transformed. His face was white now, a dull white that reflected the golden glow of the candles. Had he painted it? No, it was a skull. Sam's head was a skull!

My mind's eye jolted to the picture I'd seen of Baron Samedi, the voodoo loa. Baron Samedi wore a black suit and had a skull for a head. Somehow, Sam *had become* Baron Samedi, loa of the dead and keeper of the crossroads between the worlds of the living and the dead.

With a sick lurch of my stomach, I accepted that I had left the world of slightly scary folk tales and folk beliefs and entered another world where spirits walked the earth and your worst nightmares came true. I couldn't fight the truth any longer.

My head spun and pounded. My whole body ached in pain. In my shock, I dropped the flashlight, and it rolled away and out of sight.

52

June 18

"Finch!" Sam/Samedi commanded when he saw me. "Come here! Now you know my secret. Sam *is* Samedi. Don't you love it?"

He gave a quick laugh like a bark. "Don't you want to join my world? Why are we fighting?"

Still crouched by the cave's entrance, I pulled one of Myma's candles from my messenger bag and lit it. I didn't know what that would do, but I thought it might help somehow.

"Put out that candle," Samedi shouted, moving toward me defensively. So my instinct that the candles could be protective was correct.

Quickly, I lit another one. Holding one in each hand, I walked toward the hideous skulled figure in the dark suit. Mustering all of my courage, I repeated my earlier demand to Sam before he became Samedi: "Give me the book."

He backed away from the candles, and Caesar, still on his knees, edged sideways. The skull looked at me with its empty eye sockets. "Finch, I will kill you unless you submit to me."

Without responding, I moved closer to him. I was having trouble walking because of the pain in my legs. And I could feel my muscles shivering and moving again as though there were snakes beneath my skin.

The air was thick with heat, and sweat poured down my face and throat. The breeze I'd felt earlier had died. My hair clung to my scalp. I could feel myself getting weaker, but I kept moving forward.

"Caesar, attack!" Samedi shouted. And then he issued more commands, in a language I didn't understand.

The air of the cave suddenly came alive with the tortured spirit faces Russell and I had seen before in the graveyard. They materialized in a mist that rose from the floor of the cave, from its walls, and from the ceiling. This time it was much worse than before, though. I was surrounded on all sides by the gruesome, twisted faces that screamed from the agonies they'd experienced in life, deafening me with their horrible cries. Their sorrowful eyes tore into me like knives, and I fell to my knees, just as Caesar had.

Caesar pounded on my head and back with some implement, maybe the trowel Sam had used to kill Russell. My strength was almost gone. I hurt all over and I just wanted to sink into the cool dirt floor of the cave and be lost forever—anything to stop the pain.

I curled tightly to protect myself from Caesar's battering, still holding the candles. I sensed they were protecting me from the full power of Sam in his new incarnation as Baron Samedi. One of the candles had almost burned down, and I placed it on the floor. When I reached into my bag to replace it, I felt the bottle of milky liquid that Myma had given me. I heard her answer again when I'd asked how to use it: "You'll know when the time comes."

If there was ever a time, this must be it, I thought. My head swirled in confusion and pain. What should I do with the liquid? Should I sprinkle it like holy water? Should I rub it on my skin?

Then, as though Myma were speaking directly to me, I knew what I needed to do. Hands shaking, head still bowed to protect myself from Caesar's blows, I opened the small bottle and drank a big mouthful of the milky fluid.

It was so horribly bitter that my tongue burned as I choked it down. I groaned aloud and wanted to vomit but forced myself not to. My stomach felt like it was on fire, and my head began to spin. What was the liquid doing to me? Was I dying? Had Myma tricked me? One thing I knew: if I lost consciousness, I'd be at the mercy of Sam/Samedi and Caesar, and as good as dead.

Seconds passed but seemed like hours. With one candle burned out and the other burning low, I knew that very soon I would lose Myma's protection and be on my own against Samedi and Caesar.

As far as I could tell, the white liquid was having no effect. My thoughts were coiling bizarrely in my head, like the misty shapes in the cave. My face felt strange, and my lips and throat were thick and swollen. I hurt all over and could feel blood trickling down my neck from Caesar's blows.

There was only one thing left that I could do. "Don't be afraid to call Big Jack," Myma had said. "Don't be afraid to ask him for help; he will hear you." I didn't really believe her, but I was desperate. *I'm almost gone*, I thought. *What do I have to lose from calling Big Jack? Maybe saying his name will scare Samedi and Caesar away.*

I took a shallow breath—even breathing was painful. "Big Jack," I whispered hoarsely. "Big Jack, come save me and your book."

Nothing happened. The horrible cacophony of Samedi's spirit army continued, and Caesar's blows rained down on my head and back. I collapsed on my side, covered my face with my arms, and prepared to die.

53

Finch
June 18

I was ready to die, but instead I came alive. Gradually, I realized not only that I was still living, but also that my mind and senses were operating in a new and potent way.

The roar of Samedi's army seemed to fade into the background, even though they still surrounded me. Now, in addition to their mournful voices, I also heard the thunder and wind of the storm hundreds of feet above us. I could hear small sounds too: raindrops splashing into the salt creek, worms moving through the earth surrounding the cave, the beat of my heart, and the blood moving through my veins. All sounds seemed to be in my consciousness. It was frightening, but I also felt powerful in a way I never had before.

My sight was affected too. Colors swirled before my eyes, forming momentary shapes before splintering into shafts of light. They rose from the burning candles toward the ceiling, pulsated from the walls of the cave, and even seemed to pass through me. The African symbols on the cave walls danced and moved in response to them.

The air grew thicker and hotter than ever. Like me, Samedi was looking around, but in contrast to my state of wonder, his skull face's expression was wary. "Caesar!" he said sharply and gestured toward me. Abruptly, Caesar's blows stopped, and finally I was free from his attack.

Suddenly, a sharp blast of air extinguished the candles that had illuminated the cave. We were plunged into total darkness, but with my new senses, I could still see—first the colors that continued to swirl, gather, and break apart, and then something very different.

Forms like thick smoke began to fill my vision. Initially, I thought Samedi's ghost army was returning to haunt me, but the faces I saw this time were different. I saw Elizabeth standing in front of a lecture room at the university, writing on the board. Smiling, she turned in my direction—and changed into Myma, just as I stretched out my arms to touch her.

Now I was in Myma's tiny kitchen. Myma was brewing some kind of tea or tincture on her wood stove. She looked up as though to speak to me, and her face changed to that of an older woman whose head was wrapped in a turban.

The older woman was standing in a field with a sack over her shoulder. The field stretched for acres and was filled with bent dark bodies. Instinctively, I knew that I'd gone back in time and that these were some of the enslaved Africans who had lived on St. Pierre Island.

The Africans worked silently under the hot sun, harvesting what I guessed was rice. From the distance, a man approached them and seemed to be walking toward me. When he passed the field, some people looked up and greeted him. He signaled them in turn, without speaking.

As the man came nearer in my dream or vision, I thought I could hear his footsteps. Their regular cadence grew louder and louder... and then he was standing in front of me in the center of the cave.

I saw—or thought I saw—a man of medium height, dark brown, muscular, and strong. His face was marked with tribal scars. His expression was pitiless, like that of a god who could strike you down at any time. He was clothed in rags, and when he turned, looking about in the darkness, I saw the thick, healed marks that scarred his back and buttocks. Could this be Big Jack? A deep intuition told me that it was.

"Big Jack!" I cried out. But he ignored me. I was confused again. Was Big Jack really here, or was I hallucinating? If he *was* here, could he save me?

Big Jack strode directly toward Samedi and Caesar, his muscles rippling beneath his ruined flesh. I expected them to run, but they stood their ground and were clearly prepared to fight him.

The air of the cave was tense and charged, as though with electricity. The colors danced before my eyes. With a mighty roar, Big Jack stepped forward, grabbed Samedi around his waist, and lifted him above his head. He slammed him to the ground, dislodging rocks and dirt.

In response, Caesar rushed toward Big Jack, who brushed him aside like a bothersome fly and knocked him to the ground. Samedi rose to his feet, shouting in his strange language. At his command, the spirit army gathered and attacked Big Jack. Their filmy bodies surrounded him in misty vapor, and they savagely tore at his face and body.

The battle raged for what seemed like hours, the air reverberating with the strange shrieks and cries of the combatants. Sometimes, Big Jack shouted people's names in a hoarse voice—"Bina, Tolo!"— and I knew that he recognized them from their days together on the plantation. But they'd been brainwashed by Samedi and would not take the side of their old friend.

The cave floor shook as Big Jack singlehandedly fought off Samedi, Caesar, and Samedi's army. Sometimes I saw him fall to the ground; other times it was Samedi and Caesar. Caesar was bloodied and weakened by Big Jack's blows, but Samedi was not, because he wasn't fully human to begin with. Even when his skull head cracked loudly against the rocks, he rose again and again to clash with Big Jack's strong fists.

"Bina, Tolo!" Big Jack called out again.

This time, to my surprise, there was an effect. Some of the ghostly shapes that surrounded him retreated. They rose to the top of the cave and circled there, as though they were confused.

Suddenly, some of them descended furiously toward Samedi and Caesar. Samedi gestured angrily and shouted in his foreign language, but the haunted faces circled him just as they'd done with Big Jack—and before that with me—screeching, defiant, on the attack.

Above us, the storm raged. Beneath the grunts and shouts of Big Jack's battle with Samedi and Caesar, I also heard the gurgling sounds made by the rain as it saturated the ground around us. At the end of my strength and wracked with pain, I crouched against one of the cave walls, watching the battling forces and wondering how it was all going to end.

54

Finch

June 18

I felt like I was trapped in a dream. It seemed like I had been in the cave forever and that I would always be there. The colors, the sounds, the battle—it was overwhelming.

The gurgling I'd heard earlier got louder, and with a start I realized that water was running down the tunnel into the cave. My feet were wet, and Big Jack, Samedi, and Caesar's fight was increasingly accented with watery splashing. The cave was flooding!

Very quickly, the water rose around my ankles, forcing me to stand up, painfully.

"Big Jack, the cave is flooding," I shouted, not knowing if he could hear me, or if he even cared about such things.

He looked at me directly for the first time. His expression was remote, but not unfriendly. Strangely, even though Big Jack's lips didn't move, I heard a voice I knew was his in my head.

"Leave now," he said, "or you will drown. Take my book and destroy it."

With everything that was going on, I had momentarily forgotten about the book of secrets. Wincing from the effort of moving, I entered the cave for the first time and desperately looked for it in the rising, muddy waters. It was nowhere to be seen.

The book would float at first, I hoped, but once the cloth it was wrapped in got saturated, it would sink. How could I possibly find it?

I shuffled my feet through the water, thinking I might bump into the bundle that held the book. No luck. Then, keeping my distance from the ongoing fight, I trailed my fingers through the water, feeling for anything that was floating there. Again, I had no luck. The water was cold, gritty, and rising fast.

I wondered if I should try to escape through the tunnel. Would I still be able to get out that way? If I left now, I would be disobeying Big Jack's order to take the book of secrets, but where was it? How did he expect me to find it?

Big Jack lifted Samedi again and threw him directly against one of the cave walls with enormous force. The wall shook as though the very rock would crumble under the force of the impact.

Samedi struggled to his feet, snarling and cursing. The fracturing colors that rippled through the cave flashed across his skull face in broken prisms as he wheeled left and right, ordering the remaining members of his spirit army to attack Big Jack.

Big Jack watched him, heaving for breath but otherwise silent. His muscles were tightly gathered like those of a big cat. His features were composed and almost peaceful, except for his eyes, which glared at Samedi in the darkness like fiery coals.

As quickly as the cat he resembled, Big Jack lunged forward and lifted Samedi into the air. He slammed him into the ground near my feet so powerfully that the slippery cave floor reverberated beneath me.

In a heartbeat, the reverberation began to spread. The walls of the cave shook, and the floor shifted beneath my feet. Rocks fell from the ceiling and brought with them the painted symbols that had lasted for so many generations. The crumbled symbols floated briefly on the surface of the rising water, then dissolved into mud.

Shaken off balance, I was momentarily confused, not knowing whether this latest event was actually happening or was just another vision.

That question was answered definitively when, with a hideous roar, the cave started to collapse. The rocks and mud came from all directions, crashing on my head and throwing me off my feet into the muddy water. My head went under momentarily, and I was terrified that I would drown. Gasping for breath, I desperately struggled back to my feet. With or without the book of secrets, reaching the tunnel was my only hope for escape. I began to push my way through the deepening water. It was so hard to move forward...and I knew I didn't have much time.

I had almost reached the tunnel when, with a crash that threw me off my feet again, more rocks fell. I lunged toward the tunnel and felt frantically for an opening. It was completely closed off. There was no escape for me now.

Sobbing, I collapsed against the rocks. The rising water was almost to my knees. Soon, I would drown, and no one would know what had happened to me. I would die a lonely, gruesome death, far from the people who loved me—and all because of a book. A book I had never even held in my hands!

Sounds echoed dully off the broken walls of the cave. Dimly, I heard shouting, but saw nothing of Big Jack, Samedi, or Caesar. All I knew was that time had run out for all of us. The last thing I remembered was choking on wet earth that forced its way into my nose and mouth as my face and body were buried beneath the horrible weight of falling rock.

5 5

Finch
June 19
Heat. Waves of it radiated around me and from me.

Light. Even with my eyes closed, I was aware of the bright glare of morning sunlight.

Smells, sounds. The familiar rank odor of the salt marsh rose in my nose, while the wind gently stirred the fronds of the palmetto palms.

I was alive! I hurt all over, but apparently I had survived...what? There was too much noise and confusion in my head to remember clearly.

With a tremendous effort, I cracked my eyes open. Without turning my head, I saw the skinny legs of a water bird that was hunting for minnows. That told me I was lying near a creek. The sharp tang of earth told me the muddy shore was my pillow.

The earthy smell threatened to awaken bad memories. With a sigh, I closed my eyes again and surrendered to the pain that coursed through my body. I sank back into unconsciousness in my watery, muddy bed.

Time passed; how long? Consciousness surfaced again, and I forced myself awake. It was hotter than before, and the water was higher too. The tide was coming in. It was time to move, even though I dreaded the thought of it.

With a groan, I pulled myself up into a sitting position and dragged my body farther up on the shore of the salt creek where I was lying. All around me was wreckage—huge, downed branches, sodden grass, and dead fish. I remembered there had been a storm. When? Last night? Last week? It was all a fog.

I was glad to be alive—I guessed—but where was I? With an effort, I conquered the noise in my head and remembered that my last memory was of being in the cave.

Memories began to return, like the rising tide: strange, swirling, splintering colors; Sam's metamorphosis into Baron Samedi; Caesar's role as Sam's lackey; and, above all, Big Jack. Big Jack, who had spoken without words and told me what to do. He'd ordered me to destroy the book of secrets, but I'd never even gotten my hands on it. I guess that meant I had failed.

Wasn't the whole trip a failure? Elizabeth, Sierra, and Russell were dead, and I had come up short too. Elizabeth and Russell…the practical side of my mind told me that I would have to deal with reporting their deaths, but I didn't want to think about it. Not now. I just wanted to get back to the house in one piece. Then I could regroup and figure out what I needed to do.

All my muscles ached, but I gradually realized that it was a different kind of pain from what I'd experienced earlier. I didn't have the blinding headache, and I didn't feel like there were snakes beneath my skin. In a strange way, I actually felt better than I had before.

When I tried to stand up, I found that my legs were sore and tight, but like after a long run, not as though I was being attacked from within. That was moderately encouraging.

I crouched down on the shore, taking a personal inventory. I was still wearing my shirt and pants from the night before, but they had gotten soaked in the cave, and now they were drying in stiff, uncomfortable folds that were discolored in places with dried blood. My shoes were gone, and my bare feet were pruney from long immersion in the creek water. There were bruises on my arms and legs, and my hair and face were crusted with caked mud.

I rinsed my face as best I could in the creek water. It would dry with a salty crust, but that was better than nothing. I'd deal with my hair later.

Getting painfully to my feet, I began hobbling along the creek bank. I wondered what time it was and reflexively checked my pockets for my phone. Of course, it wasn't there; I hadn't carried it for weeks. That reminded me of my messenger bag. Where was it? Had it survived my time in the cave? I walked back to where I'd washed up and poked around in the mud with a stick.

A few inches down, I struck something solid, something that had been wedged into the muddy creek bank beneath me. Thinking that it could be my bag, I dug into the mud with my torn fingernails and then used the stick to push up more dirt. In a few minutes, I had made a good sized hole. At the bottom of it, there was a mass of muddy material. My bag? I poked and prodded more and gradually unearthed a small cloth bundle that had been partially buried beneath my body.

Was it possible?

Holding my breath, my heart pounding, I lifted the bundle and unwrapped the surrounding woven cloth, which was damp and clotted with drying mud. I peeled the layers of cloth back carefully until a small leather book was revealed within them.

Without the slightest doubt, I knew that it was the book of secrets. The real book, the one I'd last seen lying on the floor of the cave. It was in my hands at last. And I had no idea how that had happened, how it had gotten from the cave to the creek bank. For that matter, I had no idea how I had survived the catastrophic destruction of the cave either.

Suddenly suspicious that Samedi or Caesar was covertly watching me, I quickly tucked the book under my arm and looked around. There was no sign of anyone, and it was quiet—but I didn't feel safe.

I decided I would find Elizabeth's car and drive back to the house, where I could examine the book closely and safely. I wrapped it up again in the muddy cloth and stood to get my bearings.

Without shoes, it was slow going to get back to where I thought the car would be. I used the sun for guidance and walked along the shore of the creek, my bare feet sinking into the mud and sometimes painfully encountering a sharp shell or stick. Except for the soft wind, birdsongs, and the occasional plop of a fish, it was a quiet, peaceful day. Only the broken branches that littered the ground testified to the cataclysmic events of the night before.

I saw no one as I picked my way along the shore with the bundle, and I wondered again whether Samedi and Caesar had survived the cave's collapse.

I was nearing the end of my strength when I rounded a bend and saw not Elizabeth's car but Sam's truck, parked under some trees. I ran to it, hoping that the door was unlocked and that by some miracle I could get it started. I knocked broken branches off the hood and tried the door. Mercifully, it opened.

I stepped inside, catching a whiff of something that reminded me of Sam. It came from his hat, which was on the passenger seat. Did that mean he made Caesar sit in the back? I stifled a weak laugh at the thought, and hoped that Sam was the kind of person who kept his key in his vehicle.

I rifled through the glove compartment and under the driver's seat. Nothing. I sighed. Without the truck I could still walk home, but it would take a long time, and even now I didn't feel safe. I was beginning to hear strange rustlings from around the water's edge that made me nervous. I needed to get away.

Finally, I thought of looking under Sam's hat. There, neatly centered beneath it, was the key. Yes! I inserted it in the ignition and heard the sweet sound of the engine turning over. Then I locked the doors, hit the accelerator, and headed for home.

56

On the way back, I decided to stop at Myma's first. I wanted to show her the book of secrets, and I needed her advice about what to do. I turned off the main road and headed for the lane where she lived.

Myma's yard was empty when I arrived. It was midday and very hot, but the sky was clear, and there were no signs of another storm. The door was slightly ajar, and I knocked lightly.

There was no answer, and I was suddenly afraid that something might have happened to her. If Sam/Samedi had survived the cave disaster, he might have carried out his promised punishment.

I knocked again, harder, my heart pounding. There was still no answer.

Uncontrollably, I began breathing in short, hard gasps, approaching a panic attack. I peered through the door into the dim interior of the wooden house, calling out "Miss Myma! Miss Myma!" It was still and dark inside. The blue shutters were closed to keep out the heat.

My heart pounded audibly, and my spirits sank. I was convinced that Sam had killed Myma—or had her killed—because she had tried to protect me.

Then I heard a soft "Yes?" and with a rush of relief, I realized that Myma was somewhere *behind* the little house. I ran around the side and found her seated on a stool, stirring a clear liquid in a large cauldron-like pot.

"Oh, Miss Myma!" I said, as I flung myself into her soft brown arms. We held each other tightly.

"So you are safe?" she asked as we embraced, and I nodded.

Sitting with Myma behind her house, I told her the long story of the night before. She nodded from time to time and didn't seem surprised to hear about the tunnel to the secret cave, or that I'd seen Big Jack in the flesh, or that Sam turn into Samedi and viciously fought Big Jack.

When I was finished, she said softly, "Finch, do you have the book of secrets?"

"Yes," I answered and held it out to her. I had been holding it tightly the whole time I told my story.

She took the bundle from me and turned it over carefully a few times, pulling chips of caked mud off the woven cloth as she did so. "So this is it," she murmured. "This is the book Big Jack brought with him from his homeland, and this is the cloth that has kept it safe all of these years."

Stroking the cloth as though it was as special as the book it enclosed, she held it against her wrinkled cheek, closing her eyes respectfully.

She balanced the bundle on her knee and slowly unwrapped the book. Finally, it lay before us, small and bound in weathered brown leather. There were faded markings pressed into the leather cover that I recognized—with a start—from the symbols in the cave and on the candles Myma had given me. It was all coming together.

"Miss Myma—" I started to say.

"I know," she interrupted. "You recognize the symbols. They are very special. They mean nothing to you, but our ancestors understood them."

"What do they mean?" I asked, but she didn't answer. Instead, she ran her fingers over the markings as though reading them like braille, smiling to herself.

She looked up at me and said, "These symbols are part of the power of the book of secrets. They belong to our ancestors, who have been misunderstood all of these years. You are young, and you are from a different world. You were taught to study ancient knowledge, not to use it. You wouldn't understand."

Her words stung me, but I tried not to show it.

"Please, Myma," I pleaded. "Tell me about the symbols. I know I'm young, but I want to understand. After all, I came here to learn about Big Jack, didn't I?" I smiled to show that I was being lighthearted, but I hoped she knew that I was also serious.

"You see what searching for Big Jack did to Elizabeth…and Russell…and Sierra," Myma responded ominously. She looked down at the book again and slowly opened the cover.

The book opened stiffly; after all, it had been buried in Big Jack's cabin for more than two hundred years. The pages were spotted with mold but still intact, and the first few were blank.

Just as I was wondering if this book was going to turn out to be a sham like the one Sam had shown us, Myma turned to a page of strange symbols. Some were geometrical, while others were curvilinear. They resembled the symbols on the wall of the cave, but were organized in regular lines like text.

"What does this say?" I asked Myma again. "Please tell me. I want to know! I-I *want* to be more than a student. I want to be wise like you."

She looked at me somberly and said, "All right, I will tell you. And then you must destroy the book of secrets."

"What? Destroy it?" I said in dismay.

"Isn't that what Big Jack instructed you to do?" she answered. "Didn't he tell you to destroy the book?"

"Yes," I countered, "but maybe he was just afraid that Samedi would take it."

"The book of secrets is too powerful to fall into anyone's hands," Myma said gravely. "That is why Big Jack died to protect it. Do you remember the song? It is the book of life and death. It is a book of *power*, and not for Samedi, or Elizabeth, or even you or me. It must be destroyed."

"What is its power? Can you tell me that much?" I asked desperately. To be this close to the book of secrets, whatever it contained—I couldn't accept that we had to destroy it now, not after everything I had been through.

"My child," Myma answered, "there are two paths in the world, the path of love and the path of destruction. Love is the path of life, and destruction is the path of death. The book of secrets can be used for either path. In the wrong hands, it brings death. That is why Samedi wants it. He wants power, he wants death, and he wants power after death. Samedi would do anything to have power.

"Elizabeth too," she added. I took a sharp breath.

"Elizabeth knew about the power of the book?" I asked, knowing the answer in my heart.

"Elizabeth knew what was said about the book, and she wanted to use it herself. She and Samedi were alike, the two of them. Power hungry."

I shivered and asked, "What happens if the book is in the right hands? What can it do then?"

"I don't believe that's possible," Myma replied pessimistically. "People are too small and self-involved. Love is too hard for them. Destruction is too easy. That is why you have to get rid of the book. I want you to burn it. Today. I want you to do it *now*."

I was confused. "Why me? Why can't you do it?"

"I've thought about this," she replied slowly. "Because Big Jack commanded you to do it, it is your responsibility. His orders are not to be disobeyed." Myma looked over her shoulder as though she thought Big Jack might be watching us.

"Can I photograph it first?" I asked. "This is a valuable, historical book. Isn't it wrong to destroy it?"

"Go now, Finch," Myma said forcefully. "Burn the book! Then leave St. Pierre and go back to your home up North. Forget you were ever here, if you can."

She leaned over away from me and stirred her pot, then stood up. "What is that?" I asked, in a bid for time. "Is that one of your potions?"

Myma threw back her head and laughed. "Try some and tell me what you think." She dipped a chipped glass in the liquid and handed it to me. I took a sip and tasted fiery liquor that burned my throat as I swallowed.

For a moment, I thought I'd drunk another of Myma's hallucinogenic elixirs. Then I recognized the taste and the effect. "It's moonshine!" I shouted. Myma laughed again. "How do you think I support myself?" She turned serious again—deadly serious. "Finch, you have to go now. You *must* burn the book before night falls."

57

Finch
June 19

I was turning to leave when another question occurred to me. "Miss Myma, why did Sam turn into Baron Samedi in the cave?" She motioned with her hand that I should sit down again, and I felt a twinge of foreboding.

Sipping some of her home brew, Myma stared into the glass for a moment and then said softly, "Sam is not entirely from this world, Finch. He was born into it as a child, but he isn't fully human any more. Remember what I told you before: he's very old, and for years he has been studying the ancient African arts. He has powers that no man should possess. And if he gets his hands on the book of secrets, he will be even more powerful."

"Gets"—she'd used the present tense, which gave me chills. "Do you think Sam survived the cave collapse and that he's still alive?"

"Yes, I do," she said without hesitation. "The spirits he commands protect him from death. He lives partly in their world and partly in ours. He is probably wounded after the fight with Big Jack, but when he is rested, he will search for you to see if you have the book. That is why you must destroy it *now*." She pushed me for emphasis as we walked together toward the truck.

Driving home, I was weighed down by my thoughts. The people I passed were definitely surprised to see me behind the wheel of Sam's vehicle. They started to wave politely, thinking it was Sam, and then stopped in midair when they realized it wasn't. I waved anyway and tried to keep my mind focused on how much better I would feel after I had washed up and changed my clothes.

When I got to the little pink house, I was glad to see it again, even though now I was living there alone. I surveyed the rooms, seeing in them the remains of all the strange events that had taken place in the last week. In Elizabeth's room, the sheets were rumpled and stained. The air was a miasma in which the musty smell of the soiled linen mingled with the leftover scent of Myma's candles and herbs. On the floor around the bed, spent candles slumped in misshapen waxy pools. In Sierra's room, the suitcases I'd packed after she died stood by the door, ready to be returned to Chicago. In Russell's, his clothes and papers were still as he'd left them on his last day. On a table, his laptop waited patiently for an owner who was gone forever.

I closed the bedroom doors and fell, exhausted, into one of the chairs. Tears streamed down my face and I didn't even bother to wipe them away.

Russell's last day. *Yesterday.* It seemed like a million years ago. And where was he now? Lying in the ruins of Big Jack's cabin, I supposed. Hopefully, Samedi hadn't recruited him into his malevolent army. Was it realistic for me to think about going back and rescuing his body?

My troubled thoughts made my head swim and hurt. I had been so caught up in Myma's warnings about the book of secrets that I hadn't even asked her about Elizabeth's body. Eventually, I knew I would have to notify Elizabeth's family and the university—not to mention the local authorities—about her death, but what was I going to tell them? I'd have to come up with a story—but if my first responsibility was to burn the book of secrets, then everything else would have to wait. Meanwhile, I assumed that whatever process Elizabeth started after Sierra's death was moving forward.

I'd been swept up into a huge mess that I would have a hard time explaining. And if I was ever under suspicion, Myma was the only person who could speak on my behalf. *Yeah, right,* I thought grimly, *like anyone is going to believe an old Black herbalist who makes moonshine for a living.*

I decided to leave St. Pierre that very night, in Sam's truck. I would pack my things and leave everyone else's stuff behind. With Caesar gone—or so I supposed—who knew what would happen to the house and the things in it? I could always contact Myma and ask her to give everything away or something. My head spun...too many things to think about. I just wanted to eat, bathe, and get some rest before I hit the road.

I couldn't wait to go home, to see my parents again and sleep in my own bed. I thought fondly of Chicago, where houses were painted blue for decorative reasons, not to keep spirits away. Where pedestrians were assuredly people, not ghosts. And where Baron Samedi was just someone in an anthropology book.

58

But first I had to burn the book of secrets. That was very difficult to think about. I sat on my bed and unwrapped it on my lap, moving deliberately and slowly, the way Myma had done. When I'd removed all of the layers of protective cloth, I held the little book in my hands and ran my fingers over the cover, just as she had. The symbols that were pressed into the leather felt slightly warm, as though they were stirring to life.

I opened the book randomly and studied the pages. Some of the symbols on them were curved and naturalistic, while others were more geometric. Their outlines seemed familiar yet were also elusive and foreign. One was like a turtle, another like a star. Some were shaped like spirals, others more like squares. Altogether, they were distinctly different from anything I'd ever seen before. It was clear they told some kind of story, and I wanted to know what it was.

I didn't want to give the book up. But I'd promised Myma and Big Jack that I would destroy it—and if I betrayed Big Jack, would he come back and visit me? That was a frightening thought.

I also didn't like the idea of Sam/Samedi hunting me down in his search to find the book. Only Myma knew I had it, but what if he found out from her? I knew I could trust her, but I also didn't doubt that Sam could find ways to force the information out of her.

I closed my eyes so that I could concentrate better and held the book of secrets tightly, feeling its dense weight, sensing its power, wishing I knew more about its secrets. How could I come this close to ancient knowledge only to destroy it? If the book mattered so much to Big Jack that he had smuggled it with him across the middle passage, shouldn't I try to preserve it?

I was torn...so torn. Very slowly, I closed the book of secrets and returned it to its protective shroud. Then I went into the front room and laid it in the grate of the little fireplace, along with some crumpled up newspaper and pages from one of my notebooks. In the kitchen I found some matches and, with a heavy heart, used one to light the newspaper. With a pain that felt like an arrow in my heart, I watched the flames grow and begin to consume the woven African cloth. A thin trail of smoke began snaking up the chimney.

59

Finch

June 19

When I was sure the fire was well established, I went out to the pump, drew a bucket of water, and washed myself on the back porch. The water was cool and refreshing, and I began to feel rejuvenated and released from my worries and heavy thoughts. I washed my hair under the pump and twisted it up to dry. I was on my way home—to my real home! I would call my parents from Mrs. Taylor's store to let them know I was driving overnight and would arrive back in Chicago the next morning.

I checked the fire again. The African cloth was burning slowly but steadily, giving off an earthy, smoky smell. I watched the flames for a while, then finished dressing and walked down to the store.

"Mom?" My voice cracked and suddenly I was close to tears. I didn't want to start on a bad note so I sniffed and tried again.

"Mom? It's Finch."

"Finch! It's been so long since we've heard from you. Is everything okay?"

"Yeah, everything's fine," I lied. "It's a drag not having a phone signal down here. I meant to call you more often, but then we just got busy." My voice trailed off.

"Are you having a good time?"

"Um, we're learning a lot. It's really different down here from Chicago. It's almost like another world." *If she only knew.*

"You'll still be there a couple more weeks, right? Isn't it a six-week trip?"

"Actually, that's what I'm calling about. I'm going to drive home tonight. I should be in Chicago by the morning."

"Is everything okay? Why are you leaving early?"

What could I say? "Some stuff came up. I'll explain when I get home."

"Are you bringing the other kids with you?"

"Mom, I'll explain when I'm home. I've gotta go now. Love you. Can't wait to be back."

I walked back to the house, feeling a little better. Finally, I could leave St. Pierre. There were a lot of loose ends that would have to be tied up about Russell, Sierra, and Elizabeth, but I felt like I could deal with all of that later. Right now, I was focused on getting back where I belonged, safe and sound.

On the back porch, I gathered up the clothes I'd taken off earlier. Feeling something hard in the pile, I fumbled around and pulled out the bottle Myma had given me the day before. I held it up to the light and saw that a little bit of the milky liquid was still left at the bottom.

Impulsively, I drank it. I don't know why. Maybe I thought it would help me get some rest before my long drive. The bitter liquid stuck momentarily on my tongue before going down my throat like a fiery snake. I shook my head to get the taste out of my mouth and quickly drank some water. Then I packed my suitcase and collected all of our computers and notebooks.

I started to get sleepy and lay across the bed. The events of the strange summer began to play across my mind in flashbacks: our arrival on St. Pierre just a few weeks ago, when everything was new and I was innocently excited about being part of Elizabeth's research team. Tramping up and down the sandy roads with Russell and Sierra, talking to people about Big Jack. Meeting Miss Myma. Those had all been positive experiences. But gradually things had gotten darker and darker, ending with the horrifying visits to Big Jack's island.

We'd never expected that our trip to St. Pierre would turn into a life-and-death struggle. Even Elizabeth, who I knew now had been lying to us all along, could never have imagined how disastrously it would all turn out. I'd hated her for a while, but now I just felt sorry for her because greed had destroyed her. She was a brilliant researcher who had squandered her gifts in the quest for power. It was sad really. For sure, that would never happen to me.

60

Finch
June 19
I drifted off into a deep sleep. The next thing I knew, I heard voices, like people singing or chanting in a language I didn't understand. Was I awake or still asleep?

I opened my eyes and saw that I was standing on the edge of a circle of brown-skinned people who were singing in unison to drummers I couldn't see. There were both men and women, dressed in flowing garments of many colors. I didn't recognize any of them. The song they were singing was powerful and compelling, and their collective voices were evocative, even in the unknown language. The song rose and fell, interplaying in a nuanced way with the rhythmic drumming.

Even though the music, language, and people were foreign to me, I wasn't afraid. I felt at home, happy to be part of the group. The singers were slowly moving to the right, stepping in rhythm, and I fell in with them and became part of the assembly. The ground on which we danced was covered in white designs that looked like the symbols in the book of secrets. Our bare feet blurred the outlines of the designs but did not completely erase them.

The singing, dancing, and drumming continued, hypnotic and captivating. I savored the flow of the rhythm through my body and the smooth feel of the ground beneath my feet. Just as I had done that Sunday at St. James AME, I immersed myself in the collective celebration.

After a while, a woman entered the center of the circle. She was wearing a long white dress and a white headdress that contrasted beautifully with her brown skin. I could not see her face, because her back was turned to me, but I could feel that she emanated power, like a priestess.

The priestess—as I thought of her—began dancing, and the drumming and singing changed to match the rhythm of her movements. Sinuously, and with her head lowered, she moved around the inner perimeter of the circle. As she passed the other dancers, they reached out toward her, bowing their heads. When my turn came, I mimicked their actions. I hoped to catch a glimpse of the priestess's face, but she kept her head lowered. Just for a moment, she reached out and touched my hand, and something like electricity passed between us. In that fleeting moment, there was something about her that seemed familiar.

With an intuitive flash, I suddenly understood that everything around me—the songs, rhythms, dancers, and designs—was all connected with the book of secrets. Somehow, I had entered into the world of the book, and now I was getting a taste of the profound, ecstatic power that Elizabeth and Samedi had both desperately, even murderously, wanted to control.

There was power in the air, the power of life and death, of creativity and destruction.

Absorbed in the singing and drumming, I lost track of time. The dancers moved in synchrony, and together we were united in a way I'd never experienced before. The mysterious priestess stayed in the center of the circle. I understood now that she derived her power from the book of secrets. It flowed through her like electricity; it was the jolt I'd felt when she'd touched me. Her head was still lowered. Why wouldn't she let the dancers see her face? And why did I feel as if I'd met her before?

The priestess passed around the inner perimeter of the dancing circle again and stood in front of me. After the first time, she hadn't touched me—or anyone else—again. I reached out toward her, wanting to feel the electrical connection with her once more.

Instead of touching me, she slowly lifted her face to meet mine. Her brown skin, framed by the white head cloth, was smooth and ageless; it was impossible to tell whether she was young or old. Her large brown eyes were outlined in chalklike markings. More white markings, which resembled the designs on the ground beneath us, adorned her cheeks and forehead.

Previously, I had bowed to the priestess as she passed me, as the other dancers had done. This time, some instinct guided me to keep my head up, and we danced together, eye to eye, gazing into each other's faces. The rhythm of the drummers intensified, and I was aware that the other dancers had created a new circle around us as we danced together.

I felt the power of the surrounding dancers—and their love. I felt better and stronger than I ever had before and was filled by an intoxicating sense of well-being. I felt a deep conviction that everything I'd experienced in the search for the book of secrets had been worth it.

Above all, my astonishing understanding of why I danced in perfect harmony with the powerful, mysterious woman filled me with profound joy. *She was me.* She seemed so familiar because her eyes, face, and movements were mine. I was the priestess at the center of this magical world.

61

Finch
June 19

Like the breeze that signals an impending storm, now there was a subtle change in the atmosphere. The drummers shifted tempo, and the priestess quickened her step. The dancers who had encircled us reshaped into a larger circle and began moving with increased intensity. Clearly, something was about to happen.

I perceived that someone was approaching before I saw him; I heard his heavy step and felt the ground reverberate in response. Looking in the direction of the reverberation, I saw a man walking toward the circle. When he reached its outer edge, I was shocked to recognize Big Jack. He was no longer in rags. Instead, bare chested, he wore pants that were white like the priestess's dress. His expression was strong and impersonal, as it had been in the cave. His movements emanated strength and control.

The dancers parted, and Big Jack danced into the center of the circle, where he stopped, facing the priestess. His back was still hideously scarred, but his skin glowed as though it was lit from within.

Facing each other, Big Jack and the priestess began to dance together. First, they turned alternately to right and left, gradually moving toward each other until they were two or three feet apart. Then, at a signal from the drummers, Big Jack leaped into the air. When he landed, he was close enough to the priestess to touch her, but in fact only their thighs touched. Her eyes were locked on his.

They danced away from each other and then came back together again, following the cues of the drummers. They repeated this sequence over and over, their tightly controlled movements becoming increasingly sexual. The priestess rhythmically moved her hips and lower back, gently swinging her skirt, as Big Jack leaped over and over, thrusting his hips and erect penis toward her. Throughout the disciplined and deeply sensual dance, only their thighs touched— just momentarily—before the pattern began again. Meanwhile, the other dancers and I clapped in rhythm with the drums and with the priestess and Big Jack's movements.

The powerful erotic tension of their dance was another part of this enticing world of the book of secrets. "It's the book of life," the song said—and wasn't their frank sexuality the essence of life?

The drumming slowed and the circle was gradually broken. The mood changed from intense sensuality to something lighter. The male dancers took female partners and encircled them with a cloth that resembled a long scarf. The women revolved and turned as the men held the cloths around their hips. The dance was lively and their footwork was extraordinarily intricate and precise. I watched the dancers from the sidelines and saw, as well, when the priestess and Big Jack left the circle, undoubtedly to conclude what they had started.

In my heightened state of awareness, my awakened feelings flowed over and through me and understood that I was simultaneously one of the dancers who had ringed Big Jack and the priestess, and also the priestess herself, dancing with him. *Because wasn't she me?* I was no longer afraid of Big Jack. I felt his intellectual, physical, and sexual power and wanted nothing more than to be a part of it, part of his world.

Then I woke up.

62

Sam

June 19

Unfortunately, I lost my right-hand man, Caesar, last night. "Lost" sounds like I mislaid him. More to the point, he was killed when the cave under Big Jack's island collapsed. The last time I saw him, he was trapped under some fallen rocks, and the water was rising. He called out, "Massa, help me!" but I couldn't help him. I was madly trying to figure out my own escape. Big Jack hurt me in the fight, and I didn't have enough strength left to save both of us. As it was, I had to call on my spirit army for help—the ones who were still loyal to me, that is. One day, Bina and Tolo will have hell to pay for betraying me by going over to Big Jack's side. It doesn't matter that Bina was once his wife and that Tolo was his son; I'm the one they're supposed to serve now.

I'll miss old Caesar. He was very helpful to me, especially this summer when he got the idea of renting his house to Elizabeth and the students. Having them living next door made it easy for him to keep an eye on them. Thanks to him, I knew what they were up to and who they were talking to about Big Jack's song. Caesar didn't have *the power*, though, which is why he died in the cave. I have the power, but not as much as I want to have. That's why I need the book of secrets.

Even though Big Jack tried to kill me, I have always felt a special connection with him. Like everyone who grows up on St. Pierre, I heard about him and his book from the old people when I was a child. They would whisper his story when they thought our parents weren't listening.

I also felt a connection because my father's house was built on land that was part of the rice plantation where Big Jack lived. I would lie in bed as a boy, listening to the wind in the trees, wondering where Big Jack had hidden his book and what was in it. Sometimes I thought I heard voices from the graveyard, faint voices from beneath the ground that spoke of life and death. But they didn't tell me what I wanted to know about the book.

Eventually, my search for Big Jack's book took me to West Africa. That was almost a century ago, when I was a young man. I was indoctrinated there into some of the knowledge I sought, but in the end I had to return to St. Pierre to complete my quest. I was so sure I would succeed…but I haven't—not yet, at least.

Those years in West Africa were long and grueling. From plantation records, I knew that Big Jack's African name was Bemoi and that slave traders had captured him in what was now Mali. So I started my search for the book of secrets there.

I crossed the Atlantic in a battered passenger ship. I was relegated to the worst quarters because I was Black, but I kept to myself and focused on the journey ahead. Then, I made my way from Europe to Senegal and the old city of Dakar. That alone took months.

In Dakar, I shrouded myself in dark cloth like a traveler from the Sahara desert, and from there I made my way to the ancient land of Mali. For months, I traveled through remote villages. It was a very undeveloped part of the French overseas empire, and there were few roads and no cars or electricity. I learned French, Arabic, and local languages so that I could communicate with the wary, unfriendly villagers. It was very difficult…but I was determined to find the book.

At every village, I asked the elders if they had ever heard of Bemoi, a powerful man who'd been kidnapped by the slave traders. If they didn't run me out of the village, the answer was always no. But eventually, after two years of searching, my luck turned.

I was in Mopti, the ancestral home of Mali's mysterious Dogon people, known for their secret languages and symbols and knowledge of the stars. One day, I met a one-eyed man who said he could introduce me to an elder who remembered the last days of the slave trade.

The one-eyed man led me into a shadowy, circular mud structure at the back of a larger compound. When my eyes grew accustomed to the darkness, I saw a dark, wizened man who was seated on an intricately carved, wooden stool. At first the old man stared at me without speaking.

"What is it you seek?" he eventually asked in the local language.

"I'm searching for the memory of a man named Bemoi, who was stolen from these lands and brought across the sea to America. They say he was a very powerful man who knew many secrets."

Silence. Then he lifted a thin, muscular arm that was circled with gold bracelets and pointed toward the door. At first, I thought I was being dismissed, as I'd been so many times before. But instead the elder cleared his throat and said, "Walk that way for a day. Stop at the village in the shadow of Mount Hombori and ask again about Bemoi."

He cleared his throat again, which was apparently a signal, because the one-eyed man entered the small dwelling and led me out of the hut. I blinked in the sudden bright light, stepping carefully to avoid swarming chickens and children, and set out in the direction indicated by the old man's pointing finger.

Once I found the village in the shadow of the mountain, I settled in. I was not sure I was in the correct place, but for some reason it felt right. It took a long time for people to trust me, but I persevered, carefully asking questions about the history of the village and mentioning Bemoi. One day, an elderly man confirmed that Bemoi was a legendary village ancestor who'd been stolen away during the days of the slave trade. That was all he said at the time. Several months later, the elder confirmed that Bemoi had belonged to an ancient and secret cult that was the guardian of esoteric knowledge.

I was careful to conceal my excitement about this news. "How can I learn about those secrets?" I asked.

"You can only learn them by subjecting yourself to special discipline and training," he replied. "The process is severe. Not everyone survives. And if you do, you can never divulge what you have learned. These secrets must be protected with your life."

"I am willing to endure that training," I told him, and eventually I did. It almost killed me. Here's what I can reveal about it. For long periods of time, I was isolated from everyone except the other members of the cult. I was constantly tested: buried alive, tortured, temporarily blinded. I crossed every boundary that people, in their ignorance, think is fixed. I passed into the world of the dead and returned from that haunted world; I visited the past, where people move like shadows; I saw shining visions of the future. Like Tiresias, the mythic Greek, I experienced life as both a man and a woman.

And I survived. Finally, I reached the day when my initiation was completed. There were drums and palm wine, and my skin was painted with white symbols. A goat was sacrificed, and its blood was ritually scattered. I was a sworn member of the secret society. In addition, I was more than the man I'd been before, for I emerged from the training with the powers of Baron Samedi, the loa who rules the crossroads between the worlds of the living and the dead.

Now I have the power to command the dead and resurrect those who are near death. I can cure anyone of a disease, if I choose. I can hold a shriveled leaf in my hand and make it green and alive again. And I have my spirit army to do my bidding. But for all that, the book of secrets is still not mine. Why? Because the cult's elders said I was not pure. They barred me from the ultimate knowledge I sought because my African blood was mingled with that of Southward, the white overseer who fathered my mother.

So, cursing my personal history—even though it was out of my control—I returned to St. Pierre after all of those years away. My parents were long dead, and no one from my childhood was still alive, but I didn't care. I knew that there was a copy of the book of secrets on the island, just waiting for me to find it.

I moved back into my childhood home, gathered my spirit army, and waited for the right moment. In the meantime, no one on St. Pierre knew how old I was or about my time in Mali. They didn't need to. I'd found that it was better if people didn't know too much about me; I gave them only as much as they could understand. That's how I handled Caesar—and Elizabeth too.

For a few days this week, the book of secrets was mine. Finally mine after nearly a century of searching! Now, after the debacle in the cave, I've lost it again. The book that is the culmination of everything I've lived for—and suffered—for a hundred years has slipped through my fingers. Something tells me that Finch has it. Now all I have to do is find her, and the power of the book of secrets will be mine forever.

63

Finch

June 19

I'm in Sam's truck now, on my way back to Chicago. There's not much traffic at this time of night, and I expect to make good time. Finally, the nightmare of St. Pierre is behind me. I charged my phone before I left, and as soon as I crossed to the mainland it began buzzing with old texts and voice mails. I'm back to civilization!

If my parents could see me now, they might not recognize me, but I feel more comfortable with these markings on my face. I made them by mixing some of the ashes in the fireplace with water to make a nice whitish paste. With Elizabeth's white scarf around my hair, I look just right. Every time I catch a glimpse of myself in the rearview mirror, I remind myself of the priestess and I have to smile.

When I collected the ashes from the fireplace, I also rescued the book of secrets. It turned out that the layers of cloth around it were too muddy to burn well. The fire went out while I was sleeping, and the book wasn't even singed! When I get to Chicago, I'll see if I can find someone to help me translate it.

The book of secrets is safely on the seat beside me now. I'm sorry to betray Big Jack, but now that I've seen his world—the world of the book of secrets—I want more. I want to understand his world and to be a part of it. I'll need the book to do that. I'll succeed where poor, weak Elizabeth failed, and I'll fight Sam if I have to. I'll master the book of secrets, and soon, very soon, its power will be mine.

THE END

AFTERWORD

The characters in this book are fictional, but the story includes non-fictional material from my fieldwork in the South Carolina Sea Islands for the book *Hoodoo Medicine: Gullah Herbal Remedies*. The South Carolina and Georgia coasts are rich in the centuries-old folklore of the Gullah people. As I soon learned, people speak with certain—and terrifying—knowledge of ghosts that walk the lonely roads and of root doctors who can make snakes crawl beneath your skin.

In addition to my fieldwork, the text is informed by a number of historical and ethnographic sources. Sam's underground ceremony with his ghostly army and Big Jack's dance with the priestess are based on traditional Caribbean dances described in Janheinz Jahn's *Muntu; An Outline of the New African Culture*. Alfred Métraux's *Voodoo in Haiti* provided background information on Baron Samedi.

The blues song Finch hears at Sally's Club is Charlie Spand's *Big Fat Mama Blues* (accessed online at www.luckymojo.com). The sermon at St. James AME church is adapted from one described in Bruce A. Rosenberg's *The Art of the American Folk Preacher*.

George Anderson, Melvina Beckly, Margaret, and Ellen Carter, members of Sam Dent's army, were free Blacks in Virginia. Their descriptions, drawn from life, are in *Registrations of Free Negroes, Commencing September Court 1822, Book No. 2 and Register of Free Blacks 1835, Book 3*, edited by Donald Sweig.

Many thanks to Gregg and NJ, my CreateSpace editors, for their careful reading and helpful suggestions, and to my daughter, Lex Brown, whose tough questions about the story raised it to another level.

AUTHOR BIOGRAPHY

Faith Mitchell received a doctorate in medical anthropology from the University of California, Berkeley. Her work on health, society, history, and culture has been featured in a variety of publications. The Book of Secrets is her debut novel.

45837134R00141

Made in the USA
Middletown, DE
15 July 2017